The Consul's Wife

William L. Shirer

The
CONSUL'S WIFE

Little, Brown and Company
Boston • Toronto

*Published simultaneously in Canada
by Little, Brown & Company (Canada) Limited*

PRINTED IN THE UNITED STATES OF AMERICA

To John and Erna

The Consul's Wife

Chapter 1

THE MONSOON broke early that summer in Pawancore, drenching the sweltering land. There were high winds from the southwest and frequent lightning, and often the thunder drowned out the sound of the sporadic shooting in the hills above the capital and in the narrow, winding streets down by the docks.

For Harold Leighton, recovering from his latest bout with malaria, there was a healing feeling of relief at the thought that this would be the last monsoon and possibly the last tropical fever and most certainly the last revolutionary uprising, Asian or otherwise, which he would ever go through. Before the fighting was over he would be going home — this time for good.

All the other times, he reflected, going home had meant, at best, a year or two's tour of duty in Washington, but usually no more than a few weeks' leave divided between boring chores at the State Department, a quick look at the shows and shops and galleries in New York and ten days or so loafing in his native town in Illinois. Sometimes he wondered whether he would ever again get to feel at home at home. There would have to be quite a readjustment after a life spent in the foreign service mostly abroad: in Europe, in Asia and, for one somewhat hilarious interlude, in a small country in Latin America whose governments had changed faster than he could keep track of and whose constant "revolts," unlike the one out here and unlike the others he had gone through in the older continents, had been marked by a remarkable bloodlessness and by plots and counterplots on the part of bemedaled "colonels" in glittering uniforms which seemed to come right out of comic opera.

Of late he had reluctantly begun to face up to the un-dodgable fact that, young as he felt, he was entering the last stretch in a career extending over just thirty years. When he looked back at it, as he now for the first time commenced to do, it seemed to him to have been neither mediocre nor particularly distinguished. He probably would never become a Minister, as had several of his friends who had entered the service at about the same time as had he. Certainly he would never get an embassy, as had a few of the career men despite the curious and unique American custom of making ambassadors out of businessmen who gave liberally to the campaign funds of the political party in power but who possessed few other qualifications, so far as he could see, for such a difficult and exacting job.

But he had been Consul-General for five years in what

the Secretary of State, with his vast store of clichés, always referred to as one of the "key points in seething Asia." Two weeks ago word had come that he was being named a "Special Assistant to the Secretary on Asian Affairs," a title fancy enough, he mused, to impress perhaps a few Congressmen, correspondents, colleagues and pressure groups whom it would be his duty to keep out of the Secretary's hair. The post, fancy or not, might be good for the remaining five years of his service, after which he would be eligible for retirement. He would be sixty then and there would still be, he was sure, some good years left in which he and Ilka could relax, putter about and do some of the things there had been no time for all the years in official harness in foreign lands.

When he thought of Ilka his face clouded slightly and he was conscious that it must be the first time in their long and wonderful marriage that he had felt any such foreboding about her. Perhaps the fever which had kept him in bed the past fortnight had helped to augment his uneasiness. It was unthinkable that what the Governor-General himself had delicately hinted to him about her the other day was anything but pure fancy, nourished by the nightmarish atmosphere into which Pawancore had been plunged since the outbreak of violence a few months ago. Ilka had been somewhat high-strung of late, but he had put it down to the apprehension they all felt in a city gripped by a growing terror.

He might mention it in a casual way to Snow, who

would be dropping by the consulate presently to fetch him. He had already confided to his old friend that he was a bit worried about another personal problem. Isobel was rebelling too. Perhaps because she was their only child and had never had the normal childhood experience of living in one place long enough to put down any roots, Isobel had become a little spoiled. At any rate, now that she had turned eighteen, she was insisting on leading her own life, as she said. She flatly declared that she would no longer traipse along with them about the globe, like a gypsy, and that meant, she added, that she had no intention of returning home with them to enroll in Vassar, or in any other American college, in the fall. In fact — and Leighton smiled at the thought — she fancied herself madly in love with a handsome young Sikh fanatic and stubbornly asserted that she intended to remain in Pawancore and marry him.

Neither Ilka nor he had so far been able to reduce the child to reason. Perhaps Bob Snow would have some practical advice to give them. Snow had an inexhaustible source of wisdom. He was the oldest and closest friend the Leightons had; he had stood up with them at their wedding in the Rathaus in Vienna a long, long time ago. And because he knew Ilka so well, Bob might be able to help with her too.

One of the vice-consuls entered the room with a sheaf of papers for Leighton to sign. Leighton glanced at them and put them to one side.

"Anything unduly important, Willoughby?" he asked.

"I don't think so, sir," the young man said. "I did that evaluation thing they asked for — covering the situation for the fortnight you've been ill."

"I'll be interested in reading it."

"Perhaps you won't entirely agree with it, sir," the vice-consul said.

"You gave them the facts, didn't you, Willoughby?" Leighton was really quite fond of the youngster, the brightest junior officer he had had in years.

"Yes, sir. But in the evaluation part I tried to be very careful — 'on the one hand this, on the other hand that,' and all that sort of thing."

"Well, thanks very much. I'll go over it tomorrow."

As the bespectacled young man with his crew-cut blond hair withdrew, Leighton wondered what it was about this young generation that both intrigued and disturbed him. It was so typical of Everett Willoughby to emphasize how careful he had been in expressing a judgment. These youths were certainly playing it safe. They seemed to crave security. They had an unholy fear of making a mistake — however honest — that might jeopardize their careers. Was the entire generation at home like that? Leighton wondered. That would be something he would be interested in looking into when he got back.

And it would be interesting too to see how Isobel, who had grown up in half a dozen countries in Europe and Asia, would fit into her own generation at home. Though two or three of the young men at the consulate, Willoughby above all, had tried to court her, there had seemed to be an unbridgable gulf between her and them. She had not found them very interesting — even Willoughby, who had a reflective mind and, Leighton thought, a considerable charm and certainly good manners. To be sure, he was, as Isobel said, a little prim for a strapping youth of twenty-three. But that side of him would soon be rubbed off. Leighton wished his daughter were not so blind to Everett's attractive qualities. Govind Singh was attractive too, he had to admit: handsome, dashing, brilliant. But he was thirty-five and he was a Sikh, an Asian, and a dedicated revolutionary nationalist. Leighton admired him. But Singh must simply not take his daughter — that would be a disaster for her.

Leighton reached over for the vice-consul's report, glanced at it and then laid it aside. His mind seemed too blurred on this first afternoon back at the office after his illness to go to work on it. There were a dozen or so other papers to peruse and sign, but for the moment he felt too weak to tackle them.

He had had to postpone for another day an urgent meeting with his two frantic friends who represented American business out here. Both of them were having a rough time and it was one, Leighton mused, for which their previously comfortable and well-ordered lives at home had scarcely prepared them. One of the oil storage tanks which Chester Groves had recently built and filled after his company struck oil up in the hills had been set on fire by an angry mob who probably didn't appreciate the difference between a British and an American enterprise. And some nationalist fanatic with equal lack of discernment had planted a bomb in the warehouse where George Kelly kept his stock of cars and tractors, and it had exploded with considerable damage. Both men had stormed into his bedroom while he was down with malaria and demanded the protection of the flag — a destroyer or two if not a cruiser. Rightly or wrongly, the days when Washington called out the Navy to protect American property abroad were over. Besides, this dependency happened to be run by the British. Leighton had pointed this out to his two angry friends and told them that he would appeal to Lord Branhope for more protection for them. But the governor-general obviously had more pressing problems and the two businessmen, especially Kelly, a mercurial Irishman, had been on the consulate phone all day demanding to see Leighton. Temperamental and difficult as Kelly was, Leighton had taken a liking to him. He was delightfully open and frank, and he was loyal. Chester Groves was more complicated, and ever since the trouble had broken out Leighton had felt the oil man's growing hostility toward him. Groves had scarcely concealed his feeling that the American consul-general was not being energetic enough in protecting American property. He had threatened once to cable "friends" of his in the Senate about it and Leighton had told him to go ahead. Apparently, in the end, Kelly had talked him out of it.

Leighton sat back in his swivel chair, lit a cigarette, the first in a fortnight, and gazed out the window toward the harbor, where the firing seemed to have died down for the day. The British gunboat which Lord Branhope had fetched from Singapore rode at anchor not far off shore, but there seemed little activity aboard. The rain was letting up but the clouds were low, adding to the oppressiveness of the heat. He wondered how the British had endured so long in such a murderous climate. Now, after more than a century, they were getting out, or promising to. The last few weeks it had begun to look as if they might get pushed out. The nationalists were surprisingly well armed and led, and they seemed very determined — as they did these days all over this fermenting Asia. That was what had brought Bob Snow out once again. He would be writing another book about it, Leighton was sure — about The Revolt of Asia, The Approaching End of Colonialism. After all, he had been stubbornly predicting that end in the columns of his excellent magazine ever since the rise of Gandhi and Chiang Kai-shek.

Leighton rubbed out his cigarette, glanced at his watch, and then the door opened and his old friend came in.

* * *

[10]

As he mounted the hilly street toward the American consulate that afternoon, warding off the dwindling rain with his battered old umbrella, Robert Agate Snow was full of thoughts about his friend. He felt relieved that Harold was getting out of Pawancore and going home at last for good. The last five years in this steaming, turbulent place, it was evident, had taken a certain toll. Leighton had always had marvelous reserves of stamina, but he looked this time as if he had almost reached the point where he had exhausted them. Perhaps this last touch of malaria exaggerated the impression. A fortnight's fever would lay low the most robust man. But it was obvious that Harold needed a rest and a change, and it was high time that the Department, which so often seemed to be callous or forgetful of the welfare of its men in the more remote places, recognized it.

Snow felt happy too — partly out of selfishness, he admitted — that with Harold working in Washington he would henceforth be seeing a great deal more of him and Ilka than had been possible in recent years. To be sure, he reflected, there had rarely been more than a year or two's interval between his visits to them wherever they might be stationed. As owner, publisher and editor of his weekly magazine he could gallivant about the world as much as he pleased and this he did at least half the time. But these visits to his closest friends often seemed fleeting and the intervals between them unbearably long.

Sometimes he wondered why a career officer of Harold's unusual talents had not become a minister by now, or indeed an ambassador. He doubted if there were a dozen men in the entire foreign service as intelligent or as astute or as solid of character as Leighton. Moreover, though there was nothing of the pedant in him, he was quite a scholar, if that term could be divorced from the academic halls — and in Snow's opinion it could. It was not only that he had made himself a remarkable linguist — he had mastered French, Italian, Spanish, German and Russian, and for Asia acquired more than a smattering of Arabic, Urdu and Chinese. Despite his often dull and routine work at the consulates and embassies — or perhaps because of it — he had been moved to acquire what for an American diplomat was an unusual knowledge of world history, economics, philosophy and literature.

Not that these accomplishments had advanced Leighton very fast or far in the foreign service. It was not quite true to say, as he was often tempted to say, that Harold's gifts had been wasted. Certainly the American government in the practice of its world-wide diplomacy had been benefited by his contributions. But the Department had certainly never had enough imagination, or even sense, really to utilize them.

And Ilka! She had helped too. She was a strange woman and he would never, he knew, truly understand her. There were times when he wondered whether even

Harold had penetrated her inscrutable personality. Perhaps to her husband she remained a fascinating enigma too. Perhaps it was enough that he loved her. But there was no doubt that her intelligence, her poise and the baffling mystery that lay behind her dark beauty made her a great favorite in the various capitals where they had served.

Snow had known them since the beginning in Vienna. He had come to Austria after the First World War to see for his magazine whether the little country, so recently the center of the dazzling Hapsburg Empire, could survive as a small state scarcely larger than Switzerland. He was merely the foreign editor on salary at that time, but after his work was done he had fallen in love with the rococo city by the Danube, and braving the wrath of his editor at home had lingered on. One day at a party at the legation he met Leighton and immediately they became friends.

Leighton was an obscure vice-consul then, something of a gay young blade after office hours, Snow recalled, and the combination of his official position and the fresh attractive appearance of an American youth not long out of college — he was a little over six feet tall and had a thick mat of dark brown hair and eager, laughing blue eyes — made him much sought after in the fashionable though fading Viennese salons.

It was pleasant, in these ugly times, to look back on those Vienna days. Americans were generally popular then, partly because their country had rescued the city from starvation after the first war and partly, Snow remembered, because their dollar salaries allowed them to entertain rather well. Even the newspaper correspondents lived in rented palaces and maintained embarassingly large retinues of servants; and he himself had never lived so comfortably, or at least so luxuriously, before or since.

Harold Leighton, however, would have been popular without these special advantages. He looked a little like a budding poet, which was unusual for young American vice-consuls; even in those days they tended toward the prosaic business type that was so dominant at home. And his romantic air, which Snow had often envied, made him very attractive to women in a capital that was still full of romance despite all the vicissitudes of war and revolution and hunger which it had recently been through. To Bob Snow's knowledge, at least two countesses, one princess and even a Hapsburg archduchess, not to mention a rising young actress at the great Burgtheater, eyed young Leighton with a view to marriage.

He passed them all by, however, to marry Ilka. Leighton was not, as were some members of the American foreign service in those days, particularly impressed with European nobility and aristocracy. A title was scarcely a badge to turn his head. Actually, as Snow recalled, one of the countesses and certainly the young actress — later she became world-famous — were exceedingly pretty and lovely. At first the youthful vice-consul seemed quite taken by them. But they were quickly forgotten when Ilka came along.

She had shown up one day as a translator and interpreter in the consulate, and though her competence was conceded even by the aging consul-general himself, she quickly disrupted the staid office over which he presided. There was something about her, Harold Leighton confided to his friend after the first week, which made it impossible for a man to get on with dry reports for the State Department while she was around.

What was it? Harold was obviously too smitten to be very articulate.

"You can't describe it. You've got to see her, and feel her presence there in the room. I tell you, Bob, it's shattering," Harold had muttered. "She is beautiful, yes. And intelligent and sensitive . . ."

"Vienna is full of beautiful women," Snow had interrupted. "And they are all intelligent and all sensitive and . . ."

"You don't get me," Harold had cut in impatiently. "Of course Vienna is full of attractive women. We all know that. But Ilka is different. She's . . . she's beyond them all, I tell you. She's . . . Well, confound you, you'll have to see for yourself."

Bob Snow had seen for himself a few evenings later when the three of them dined at Sacher's. He gazed in wonderment across the table at the dark, strange woman and was immediately fascinated and captivated. There was so much to take in. There was a tantalizing beauty in the lovely white skin set off by the jet-black hair; in the subtle curve of her neck and the soft contours of her shoulders; in the finely chiseled nose, which was straight but gave the impression of turning up slightly and defiantly; in the eyes, which were unusually wide apart and jet-black like her hair, and brooding, so that they exuded an air of some unfathomable mystery of personality and purpose.

A man could note in his mind these features and a dozen others and add the low, warm voice and the way the face would light up and the eyes sparkle and then how a sadeness would creep upon them. But there remained a great enigma and it was this, Snow felt, which made Ilka in those first hours, as she did today, a quarter of a century later, inspire in one a great and noble longing that would never be quenched.

Leighton had not mentioned her nationality, but Snow knew immediately from her slight accent that she was Hungarian. She had been, it came out during their talk, a student at the University of Budapest, majoring in languages and concentrating on English, but she had fled the terror which gripped Hungary during the chaos that followed the end of the first war and had made her way to Vienna without finishing her studies.

"The red terror or the white?" Snow asked.

For a moment, he still remembered, Ilka had gazed at him searchingly with her lustrous black eyes.

"Both," she said quietly. "They were equally barbarous. And one was as tyrannical as the other."

Though he did not realize it until much later, this was the first clue Ilka ever gave to them of a view of life that they would only fully comprehend, after so many years, at the summer's end in Pawancore.

Bob Snow was always thankful that back in the Twenties there was no silly ban, as there later was, on American diplomatic and consular officials marrying foreign women. Two months after he had first set eyes on her in the consulate office, Harold Leighton married Ilka in a simple ceremony at the Rathaus in Vienna. The Burgomaster himself, a genial old soul with a white goatee which made him look like a portrait painted by Vandyke, performed the ceremony. Snow and the consul-general's wife stood up with the handsome couple as witnesses, and after a pleasant wedding feast at Sacher's, Harold and Ilka caught the Arlberg Express for a month's honeymoon in the Tyrol.

Not long after his return to work, Leighton was transferred to Prague, and Snow, who still remembered how empty and barren Vienna suddenly became for him after his friends departed, left for home. But in the ensuing years, especially after he gained control of his weekly magazine and was free to wander about, he saw them on and off in various capitals: Prague, Oslo, Berlin, Paris, London, Madrid, Rome, Moscow, Cairo, Delhi, Bangkok, Shanghai and Peking. They were a popular couple in the diplomatic-consular circles and they got along wonderfully together. Their devotion to each other seemed to Bob to be without limits and certainly without reservations. In Vienna in the early days he had discerned an inner restlessness in Ilka — it was said to be common in Hungarians — but as she grew older she appeared to discipline it; and perhaps the moving about from one capital to another every two or three years helped to exhaust it. All the years he had known them, their marriage continued to grow in depth and harmony. Snow, whose own marriage had quickly gone on the rocks, often envied them. Their union seemed blessed by the kindest and rarest of fates.

And yet — as he made his way up the steps to the consulate in Pawancore that rainy afternoon after watching a rather messy attempt by a platoon of British police to flush out a nationalist snipers' nest near the docks, Snow wondered whether for the first time in his life he had not detected an undertone of uneasiness in Harold about his wife. He did not like to admit it, and perhaps it was due entirely to the depressed spirits one fell into, as Harold had, during a malaria attack. Once or twice though, during the fortnight he had been here, he thought he had recognized in Ilka a return of her old restlessness. Or was it merely an understandable impatience with her daughter for stubbornly insisting on carrying on with that young Sikh lawyer? That and her equally understandable impatience with the governor-general for calling off negotiations with the nationalists and resorting to armed force to put them down? The bloodshed of the past few weeks had made her sick and one evening at dinner she had damned old Branhope with a vehemence which had surprised Snow, though his sympathies too, and even those of Harold, were with the nationalists, who, after all, as he never tired of saying, wanted only what Englishmen had had for centuries: independence.

Well, he would try to steer their conversation away from such matters for the time being. Harold needed all his strength to recuperate from his illness and wind up his affairs at the consulate and get packed for going home. Snow greeted the doorman, handed him his dripping umbrella and mounted the stairs to Leighton's office on the second floor.

Chapter 2

Despite his feebleness and the suffocating heat, Leighton, to his friend's surprise, was in no hurry to leave the office. Snow found the place sweltering. He had really come by to make sure that Harold did not overtax himself by working late on this first day back at his desk. He would have preferred to depart immediately for the Leighton villa, where Harold and Ilka were putting him up during his stay. Lying up in the foothills behind Pawancore City, the villa would be at least ten degrees cooler and there might be a refreshing breeze from the bay. They could sit out in the garden — or on the veranda, if it started to rain again — and sip their highballs and relax. But Harold made no move to go.

"It's probably against regulations," he said, forcing a hint of a smile on a face still haggard from fever, "but I always keep a little stuff here. Besides, Bob, you look as if you needed a drink — quick."

Snow had not been aware of it, but now he saw that his Palm Beach suit was drenched — outside from the rain and inside from perspiration — and that it hung on him like a sodden sackcloth.

"Well, let's say we both need one," he grinned. "But wouldn't you prefer, Harold, to take it at home — with Ilka?"

Harold answered by ringing for someone, and a moment later a bearer slipped in on bare feet with a pail of ice, a bottle of Scotch and some soda water. As Leighton poured the drinks and they took a first gulp, Snow was struck by how worn-out his friend seemed.

"You really shouldn't have come to the office today, Harold," he said.

"I might just as well not have — for all the work I did."

"You mustn't kill yourself — these final few weeks, you know."

"I know. But things pile up when you're away," Leighton said, pointing to the stacks of papers on his desk. "I didn't have the strength to wade through them."

"They can wait," Snow said, emphatically.

"But my business friends can't. Both Groves and Kelly have been on the phone all day."

"What do they want, the U. S. Navy?"

"Nothing less," Leighton smiled.

"Wouldn't old Branhope have a fine fit — if he saw a U. S. cruiser, or even a destroyer, steaming into the bay!" Snow exclaimed, with a chuckle.

"He would probably request it to leave by sundown

and protest to me about American effrontery in trying to interfere in a purely British affair. Not that he couldn't use a cruiser, Bob."

"I doubt if a battleship would help much now. Things have gone too far. Doesn't Branhope realize it?"

"If he does, he won't admit it."

"The last of the old proconsuls! But he has his points," Snow added.

"Yes. Courage and courtesy and a granite integrity, according to his own lights."

"The trouble is he was born too late," Snow said. "He belongs in the nineteenth century."

"With that remarkable breed of proconsuls the British produced in those days — the greatest since the Romans," Leighton added.

He had been fascinated by his studies of them, in Egypt and India above all, where they had risen to the greatest heights — Cromer, Milner, Ripon, Lytton, Lansdowne, Morley, Minto, Zetland, Curzon — and he had recognized Lord Branhope as a genuine successor to them and admired him for the qualities that had come down with a great tradition. Unfortunately, the tradition had not kept up with the changing times, with the reawakening of the East, and there had been more than one occasion in the last five years when Leighton had reminded the Governor-General of that and pled with him to consider the unavoidable consequences of the twentieth century.

"They had greatness," Snow said. "But to emulate them today, as Branhope is trying to do, is not greatness but foolishness." He was beginning to enjoy the talk and the drink. He could feel his friend relaxing just a little. But a moment later he saw Leighton's eyes darken and his jaws twitch and tighten.

"Branhope came to see me the other day," Leighton said, "while you were out."

"He did? While you were ill?" Snow was disturbed to hear it. "I'm surprised Ilka let him in, seeing that you were pretty delirious and in no shape to talk to anyone."

"I wasn't feeling too bad, actually. The old boy seemed genuinely concerned to see for himself how I was and to express his regrets at my going. Rather decent of him, I thought."

"Rather inconsiderate, I'd say," Snow snorted.

"Branhope had something else on his mind," Leighton said, after a pause. "That concerned me, I mean."

"What was that?" Snow tried to sound unconcerned.

"That's what I wanted to talk to you about, Bob — away from Ilka."

It was the first time, Snow reflected, in their long friendship that Harold had ever said that. Ilka had always been such an intimate part of their life together that he could not recall an occasion when she had purposely been excluded from their conversation.

"Well, if we're going to linger here, I'm going to take off my coat," Snow said, rising and slowly unbuttoning it. The heat was stifling, despite the thick walls of the old consulate building, but Snow was conscious of making a gesture of annoyance in the vain hope of perhaps throwing his friend off his thoughts until another time, when he would be stronger and perhaps see things less darkly than today. But Leighton did not respond.

"And you're going to have to pour me another drink, Harold," Snow added, "with a lot of ice in it. It's damnably hot here, you know." He flung his crumpled, sweaty coat over a chair.

Leighton filled both their glasses.

"You've met that young Singh fellow at our house," he began, lighting a cigarette and blowing smoke rings toward the ceiling.

"Yes, and at his office. And I must say, Harold, his affair with Isobel aside, if it is an affair, I find him an attractive young man. A bit of a fanatic, to be sure, like most of these nationalist rabble-rousers. But he strikes me as a very shrewd lawyer who knows what he's after."

"I like Singh too, though not for Isobel," Leighton said softly, and the twinkle in his eye was reassuring to his friend.

"He certainly isn't serious about marrying her, is he?"

"I don't know," Leighton said. "I hear only Isobel's side. She seems to be damned serious. But I won't have it, I tell you."

"It would be a mistake, I agree," Snow said.

"Mind you, Bob, it is not on racial grounds that I oppose it. It's just that Isobel is too young, and that they come from different worlds."

"Singh, I must say," Snow said, "strikes me as having much too much on his mind these days to spare much thought to courting an American teen-ager, attractive as Isobel is." The more Snow thought of it, the more he thought his friend was exaggerating the whole affair.

"Singh has a great deal on his mind these days," Leighton said. "Do you know what the governor thinks?"

"What?"

"That Singh may be the real leader of the terrorist wing of the whole nationalist movement."

"I doubt that, Harold. He's much too intelligent and, I might add, much too fond of good living — on a Western scale — to risk his neck in any foolishness."

"I'm not so sure," Leighton said. "Sometimes he strikes me as being so fanatical about achieving this country's independence overnight that he would do anything. Cut your throat or mine, even, if we stood in his way."

"Surely you exaggerate, Harold," Snow said, smiling as breezily as he could. "I agree with you, though, that in the present circumstances Singh is hardly the proper suitor for the innocent daughter of the departing American consul-general. But honestly, Harold, I don't think there is anything to worry about on that score."

"I'm much more concerned, Bob, with something

else," Leighton said, and the gravity of his face and his voice startled Snow.

"Don't you think it's time we were getting on home?" Snow said quickly, trying to forestall his friend. "I promised Ilka I would deliver you early today. And it's getting late."

Outside, he noticed, it was getting dark, the night coming on quickly as it always did in these equatorial places. He got up to peer through the window. The street lights were sparkling here and there in the city just below.

"This is a curious revolution, I must say" — he turned back to Leighton, who had remained motionless in his swivel chair — "when the power plants continue to function."

Leighton was buried in his thoughts and did not answer. Snow stood before him at the desk. "Shall we be getting along?" Snow proposed again.

"In a moment," Leighton said softly. Behind his great patience was a determination that his old friend at once recognized. Snow sat down.

"I can only say it here, Bob, and to you alone. I'm concerned about Ilka. And as you must know, for the first time, I think, in our lives."

"Her health, you mean?" The obvious thought popped into Snow's mind: a killing cancer. But they wouldn't have hidden such shocking news from him.

"No." Leighton stared at his friend for a moment.

"Bob, it is just possible that Ilka may be mixed up in this thing."

"In what thing, for God's sake?" Snow said sharply, leaning forward impatiently.

"That is really why Branhope came to see me, I think," Leighton said. "About Ilka."

"Well what about her, for God's sake!" Snow fairly barked.

"He was very delicate and diplomatic about it, naturally. The very mention of it was as painful for him as for me. He said he had got a report from his C.I.D.* that Singh may have beguiled Ilka into more than an innocent interest in his work."

"Ilka Leighton, of all people! How ludicrous! For God's sake, Harold, are you out of your mind?" In his exasperation Snow jumped up and began pacing the floor. "Of all the absurd, asinine things I ever heard!"

"I'm not saying I believe it, Bob," Leighton said.

"Well, I should think not!"

"I want to be fair about it. The governor assured me he didn't believe it himself — it was too absurd to take seriously."

"Then why did he trouble you about it — being the gentleman of the old school that he is?"

"Because," Leighton said, "rumors like that invariably reach the American consulate, usually in a highly exaggerated form, and he wanted, he said, to spare

* Criminal Investigation Department, the secret police.

[27]

me embarrassment — put me on guard, so to speak."

"Harold," Snow said warmly, "you are much too wise and experienced to waste your time mulling over rumors — especially the idiotic ones."

"But this one does make me uneasy, my friend," Leighton said. "You can understand that, can't you?"

"No, I can't. In fact, Harold, I think the whole thing is a figment of your delirium. You were quite out, you know, several times during that malaria. I'll check with Ilka, but right now I doubt if the governor even came to see you. It was just something you imagined during one of your feverish nightmares."

"He came to see me, all right," Leighton said.

"Well, maybe Branhope was delirious and should have been home in bed taking care of himself."

Snow paused before the window and looked out. There was a faint outburst of rifle shots from the dock area. A searchlight from the gunboat offshore played back and forth but there was no return fire. Snow came back to the desk and sat down.

"Honestly, Harold," he said. "I wouldn't give it another thought."

"You haven't noticed her restlessness?" Leighton asked.

"Ilka used to be a little restless. It was in her rich Hungarian blood. But she got over it, didn't she?"

"Yes. She seemed to exhaust it in the nomadic life we led."

"You're all a little high-strung after what you've been through the last few weeks, Harold," Snow said. "But now that you're getting away from it there is nothing to worry about."

"I was never much of a worrier, you have to admit."

"That's it. That's one reason, Harold, why you were always so effective in this thankless job of yours. Why begin now?"

Leighton smiled but said nothing.

"Incidentally, Harold," Snow said, trying to break the tension, "if any member of the consul-general's family is mixed up in this thing with Singh, it would be Isobel, wouldn't it? She is young enough and innocent enough to have romantic ideas about political terror, or at least about political terrorists risking their lives in a noble cause."

"Isobel is completely innocent — I'm convinced of that," Leighton said. "She hasn't the faintest idea of what Singh may be up to."

"Well, to be frank, neither have you, Bob. At least you have no evidence, have you?"

"No," Leighton conceded after a pause. "But I feel the governor may have some. After all, he has a secret police."

"The most inept I've seen in all Asia!" Snow exclaimed. "What's more, it's honeycombed, I believe, with nationalists who purposely flood it with rumors from the bazaars — like this imbecile one about Ilka —

to confound the authorities. That's happening in all the countries out here. It is part of the breakdown of the white man's rule. He can no longer depend, as he once did, on his secret police. And I doubt that here in Pawancore the governor can depend much longer on the rest of his native police, or even on his native troops."

"I agree," Leighton said, somewhat relieved to find agreement with his friend. "And I've told him so."

"But he won't listen, will he?"

"It's a difficult thing for him to believe. After all, British rule all over Asia has depended for the last half century at least on the use of native police and troops. Still, he told me the other day he is determined to put this thing down if he has to get a division of infantry and tanks out from England."

"I doubt if that would be enough, even if they had a division to spare at home, which they haven't," Snow said. He was glad to get the conversation off his friend's personal worries and onto a subject he himself was full of, for he was writing reams about it in his dispatches and in the notes for his book. "Branhope probably can clean up the docks and even the rest of the city with what he has. But outside the capital he has already lost. Try going up north into the hills. Ten miles out, as I found out the other day, His Majesty's rule ends. The nationalists have taken over."

"I suppose it was inevitable," Leighton said. "But

still, Bob, this bloodshed is a great pity. The British have promised, after all, to get out."

"Why don't they then?" Snow answered quickly.

"It takes a little time, Bob. You can't blame them for wanting to leave the place honorably — and leave it intact."

"With law and order, and all that sort of thing. God, Harold, aren't you weary of all their pious talk about 'law and order'?"

"Well, it's something the British brought to these parts," Leighton said, "and on the whole it has been pretty admirable."

"The conception perhaps, but not the practice," Snow suggested. "I don't think the people of Pawancore, or of India, believe there has been much justice under the British — at least of the kind an Englishman enjoys at home. If there had been, the jails and the prisons would not have been so jammed with political prisoners for the last quarter of a century."

"At least the British didn't hang them or shoot them, as the Japanese and the Russians would have done," Leighton retorted.

"They did at first. But they've grown more humane, we have to admit."

"It's something we often overlook," Leighton added.

"As for the order you speak of, yes. There has been order until recently," Snow said. "But aren't slaves usually orderly, until they become desperate and armed?"

"You dwell in the past, my friend," Leighton smiled. "Within two or three years these people will be free."

"It may seem like a long time to men like Singh," Snow said.

They could hear the shooting down by the harbor flaring up. A machine gun on the gunboat started to blaze away. Snow got up and went to the window to watch the flashes in the sky. He heard the telephone ring. It was Ilka, and Leighton was telling her that they would be along presently.

In the consulate car going home, Snow could feel his friend tightening up. He was obviously absorbed with his personal problems again.

"You know what I'm going to do, Bob?" he said, as they neared the villa.

"What?" Snow said, as casually as he could.

"Three things," Leighton said determinedly. "First, I'm going to call in that young Sikh firebrand and break up whatever is between him and Isobel. Then I'm going to sound him out about Ilka. Finally — and, believe me, it will be the most painful moment we've had together in twenty-five odd years — I'm going to put it up to Ilka."

"Put what up to Ilka?" Snow said acidly.

"What the governor said."

Chapter 3

He had begun with Isobel.

One evening a few days later Bob Snow volunteered to escort Ilka to an evening reception at the French consul-general's and Leighton had taken advantage of their absence to speak with his daughter alone. A busy father, he reflected, harassed so much of the time by pressures which came in a job like his, rarely had such an opportunity, and as he looked at her now, curled up on the divan calmly smoking a cigarette, he saw that Isobel had grown up, had become a woman, without his having fully realized it until this moment. For too long, out of sheer habit, it must have been, he had regarded her as a delightfully awkward adolescent. At some time during the last year, as she was approaching eighteen and while his mind was preoccupied with the outbreak of trouble in Pawancore, she had slipped into womanhood. A year or two before, he had been relieved to see her shedding her plumpness and a sort of adolescent gawkiness. But only now it was plain to him that, as he had hoped, she was going to resemble rather strongly her mother, possessing the same trim figure and a dark and intriguing beauty and the same poise, but exuding as well, Leighton was glad to see, an air of innocence which her mother may never have had, even at eighteen.

There had been a slightly awkward moment of silence between them after Ilka and Snow had departed, and then Leighton, lighting his pipe and leaning back comfortably in his chair opposite the divan, had broken the ice.

"Isobel, are you glad we're going home?"

"For your sake, Father," she said.

"My sake?"

"I mean, I'm happy about the promotion, and all that."

"But I'm thinking about you, my dear," Leighton said, smiling. "One of the things, Isobel, that always weighs on the conscience of a foreign-service officer is that his children have to grow up away from home."

"I like it here," she said, looking away.

"This new appointment," Leighton said, deciding not to take notice of her retort, "means for one thing, Isobel, that you can start in Vassar this fall. I think this time we will be in Washington long enough to see you through your four years there."

"But I don't want to go to Vassar, Father," Isobel said — "or to any other college at home, for that matter."

"What on earth do you want to do then?" Leighton asked, trying to sound more genial than he felt.

"Stay here!"

Leighton, watching her dark eyes, her mother's eyes, blaze up, paused to relight his pipe, though it had not gone out, and to consider quickly his next step. He might as well, he decided, get to the heart of the matter at once, now that Isobel had given him an opening.

"My dear girl," he said somewhat sternly, "can I be frank with you?"

"Why not?"

"This affair of yours, Isobel, is simply out of the question."

"What affair?" she asked, gazing at the ceiling.

"With Singh. Understand, Isobel, I do not object to him on racial grounds. Whatever prejudices I may have had in the past on that score I have shed since I came out to Asia. It is simply, my dear girl, that two people with such tremendously contrasting backgrounds can't possibly make a go of marriage — even if he were not nearly old enough to be your father. You understand that, don't you?" Leighton felt relieved to get it off his chest.

Isobel did not answer at once. She reached for an ash tray, rubbed out her cigarette, took a fresh one and fumbled with the lighter.

"What if . . . perhaps," she said hesitatingly . . . "I . . . love him?"

[35]

"Do you think he loves you?" her father said, feeling immediately a little ashamed for putting what to her must have seemed a savage question. But he was determined to rescue this innocent child, no matter how much it hurt her for the moment. A year hence she would be grateful to him for opening her eyes.

"I think so," she said softly.

"Naturally," Leighton said, "Singh is flattered that a young girl of your beauty, of your color of skin —"

"Stop!" she cried, sitting up with a jerk and staring angrily at him. "I never expected you to say such a mean, low thing!"

"All right, my dear," Leighton made quick to answer. It was the first time his daughter had ever spoken to him like that, but what hurt him most was that he knew she was more than justified. "I told you I had no racial prejudices in this matter, and I haven't. What I'm trying to say, Isobel, is that naturally Singh feels flattered by the attentions of a pretty young American girl. It's only human."

"Pawancore is full of beautiful Hindu and Sikh women," Isobel said, recovering her composure. "You must have noticed it yourself. Or are you blinded to beauty in a brown skin?"

"Of course not!" Leighton said emphatically. He had, in fact, been struck by the loveliness of some of the Pawancore women. Quite a few of the educated ones, or the wives of educated husbands, and even occasionally an illiterate village woman whom he had noticed in his tours of the countryside had an indescribable gracefulness and often haunting faces, full of passion. He had admired them aesthetically, as a painter might, but he had not been personally attracted to them. One really did not get to know them; no consular or British official would have thought of crossing the color bar. One met these women with their husbands at official functions but they seemed timid and retiring and Leighton had found it difficult to make conversation with them.

A handful of Sikh and Hindu Westernized intellectuals who had studied in England or on the Continent had brought back English or Continental wives, and one professor of philosophy at the university, Krishna Maliviya, had returned from a year's teaching at Harvard a year or two ago with a young wife from Boston who had become a good friend of Isobel's and who, Leighton now began to suspect, might be secretly encouraging his daughter in her folly. The Maliviyas, Leighton realized, were a bad example for an impressionable youngster like Isobel. They seemed to be deeply in love and to be extremely happy and harmonious, though he wondered how it would be when the mixed children came. Actually, Leighton was greatly attached to Professor Maliviya. He was one of the few persons in Pawancore with whom he could discuss philosophy; and from him he had drawn the inspiration and the encouragement to pursue his own desultory studies of Hindu and Buddhist thought.

Lost momentarily in the thoughts which Isobel's sarcastic question had provoked, Leighton did not hear his daughter speak up.

"I asked," Isobel said, "what you have against Singh — besides the color of his skin?"

"For the tenth time, Isobel," he replied with some annoyance, "I tell you I have nothing against his color. Please believe me! I would say, my dear — if I may sum up — that there are three compelling reasons why this thing is out of the question. First, as I said, the difference of age — he's thirty-five and you are just eighteen. Then there is this immense gulf between your backgrounds. You could never really bridge it. There's a third consideration . . ." He paused a moment.

"And what is that?" she asked.

"Do you have any idea whatsoever, Isobel, what Singh is up to these days?"

"I know he is frightfully busy at his job."

"Practicing law?"

"Yes. You yourself, Father, have often said he's the busiest lawyer in town. He seems to work frightfully hard at it."

"He did — until recently," Leighton said. "But, my dear girl, there's a revolution here, as you know. And I have reason to believe that Singh is up to his neck in it."

"He is?"

Isobel said it so innocently that Leighton felt confirmed in his belief that she had no suspicion of what her handsome friend was up to.

"My point is, darling," Leighton said, feeling that he was driving it home triumphantly, "that for the time being Singh is so preoccupied with his part in this struggle for independence — whatever it may be — that he will have no time or thought for you, or for any other woman. Unless you want to get mixed up in this thing with him. And for a foreign woman, that is out of the question."

"I don't see why," Isobel said. "You say yourself that all these people want is to be free and independent, like ourselves. I don't see why it would be wrong for me to help, if Singh wanted me to."

"Well, in the first place, Isobel, a foreign woman, and especially a Westerner, has no business interfering in it. And in the second place, it's not child's play. A lot of people are getting shot, and some of the leaders, if they persist in their terror, may get hanged."

"Hanged!"

"Yes, the governor is getting tough."

"He's a horrid old man," Isobel said, puckering her lips, and Leighton marveled at her girlish innocence.

"He is in a difficult position, and he is doing, no doubt, what he thinks is right," Leighton said.

"Do *you* think he is right?" Isobel asked. "Killing all these people?"

"Well, both sides are killing people. Force always begets force, Isobel."

They had drifted into a talk about the uprising, and Leighton, stimulated by his daughter's rapt attention, delved into it so deeply, trying to set it for her in the historical framework of an Asia that, exhausted, had been asleep for centuries and was now awakening and stirring, that he forgot the purpose he had had in mind all evening. Catching himself up at last and glancing at his watch, he returned hastily to the subject.

"Well, that's what is happening here, Isobel, and, as you see, it's a microcosm of what is going on all over Asia."

"I really had no idea," Isobel said. "I'm really a very ignorant person, aren't I?"

"Not for your age, my dear. But college at home will, shall we say, broaden your knowledge."

"But I didn't say I was going home to college, Father," Isobel smiled.

"I'm afraid I shall have to insist on it, darling," Leighton said.

"We shall see," she said.

And that was as far as the consul-general got. Once, just before Snow and Ilka returned, he turned the conversation toward his young and brilliant vice-consul.

"What about this young Willoughby?" he asked. "I rather gather that he has taken quite a fancy to you. How do you feel about him?"

"Neutral," Isobel replied, breaking into a grin.

"Personally," Leighton said, "I've taken a great liking to him. He is the most brilliant youngster I've had at the consulate in years."

"Everett is nice," Isobel said. "I like to have him around, especially for tennis. But, Father, since you ask — he is just not very exciting . . . the way Govind Singh is. He's so . . . so . . ." She searched for the word.

"So what?" Leighton asked impatiently.

"So immature," she said.

"He's twenty-three years old," Leighton protested — "and a graduate of a good university; Princeton, I believe."

"That's just it, Father," Isobel said, smiling.

Then Ilka and Bob Snow had come in from the French party and Isobel, obviously relieved to escape further efforts of her father to pin her down, vanished to her bedroom. Snow too had soon retired, leaving Leighton and his wife alone in the big living room.

"Would you like a nightcap, dear, before turning in?" Leighton asked.

"I would love one, darling," Ilka said eagerly, and it occurred to him as he made the drinks that she, who had always been a more moderate drinker even than he, had been outdoing him of late. She must have had a highball or two at the French consul-general's and ordinarily that would be her limit for one evening. As he looked at her now, feeling tender with the love that her mere presence always stirred deep within him, her cheeks seemed to him to be a little flushed. The slight coloring though, he thought, became her in the soft light of the lamplit room. Tomorrow, by day, in the glaring tropical light, the skin would be gleaming white again against her glistening coal-black hair. How little, he thought, she had changed in appearance over the years. There was still no trace of a graying hair, the nose was still as straight and pert as the first day he had glimpsed her in Vienna, the pure-black eyes sparkled just as brightly, the figure was just as neat, the curves of her neck and shoulders as soft and subtle. The years, in fact, he saw, had merely ripened her beauty so that now it seemed to him to be in full bloom, without a flaw, as was her whole being, at least until the recent weeks. There was another thing, he mused, that the passing of so much time had left unchanged: the enigma of this woman. He had never really penetrated it and now, he supposed, he never would. He no longer felt frustrated at this failure, he told himself, if it was a failure. For years he had recognized that the mystery at the core of Ilka's personality formed part of the magnet that drew him ever closer to her, and that to solve it might be a disaster for both of them. Love itself, the deepening, unquenchable kind he had been lucky beyond most men in having, was enough, and long ago he had abandoned as futile and indeed undesirable the attempt to

[42]

analyze it and to search in his mind for the source of many of its hidden springs.

"Lost in your thoughts again?" he heard her say.

"I was thinking of you, my dear," he said. His revery, he saw, must have lasted several minutes. "Of how beautiful you are, despite all our years, and of how much I love you."

She looked at him tenderly, her eyes lighting up like glowing coals, her full mouth curling into a warm smile, but for a moment she said nothing.

"Did you and Isobel find a lot to talk about?" she asked after a while.

"I did most of the talking," Leighton smiled. "I told her she would have to forget Singh — that the whole thing was out of the question. I'm afraid I was a little hard on her. She fancies herself in love with him. Well, I suppose he is an attractive fellow. You find him so, don't you?"

"Yes, I do," Ilka said.

"But you agree with me, don't you, that the thing is quite impossible?"

"Now that we're leaving, Harold," Ilka said, "won't that settle it?"

"It may precipitate it!" Leighton was a little surprised that Ilka took it so calmly. "Singh may try to marry her before we go — if only to keep her here."

"I'm confident, Harold, it won't come to that."

"How do you know?"

"I think I know," Ilka said, and the tone of positiveness in her resonant, low voice, reflected as it was in her eyes and hinting at a knowledge that was beyond his and that she would not share, instead of reassuring him stirred a pang of uneasiness in him.

"Isobel hasn't the faintest notion," Leighton said after a moment, "what Singh is up to these days."

"Have you?" Ilka asked quietly.

"I haven't had a chance to tell you because of so many other things on my mind at the office, but the governor believes, Ilka, that Singh may well be the secret leader of this nationalist terrorist gang that is starting to raise hell all over the place." Leighton watched closely for his wife's reaction.

"It sounds unlikely, doesn't it?" she said, and he could discern no change at all in her eyes nor in the low, soft tone of her voice. Her sincerity seemed so obvious to him that he quickly squelched the urge to go on and take the plunge and confront her with what old Branhope had said about her. He was becoming convinced, in fact, that Bob Snow was right and that there was nothing in it. In the end, perhaps, he would have to mention it if only to erase it completely from his mind. Tomorrow Singh, whom he had arranged to see, might give him some clue, one way or the other.

"I'm not so sure," Leighton said, bringing his mind back to her remark. "Singh strikes me as a fanatical fellow who will shrink at nothing. He may well have contrived the business of setting Groves's storage tank on fire and planting that bomb in Kelly's warehouse. At least the governor thinks so."

"I should think," Ilka said, "that Singh is concerned these days with more important things."

"What do you mean?"

"It seems to me, Harold," Ilka answered, "that the terror here is quite above ground, with nothing secret about it. It's in the fighting down by the docks and up in the hills, in the massacring of Hindus and Sikhs by your Lord Branhope's police and troops."

"The killing isn't all on one side," Leighton said.

"Yes, these people fight back — but with what?"

"They seem surprisingly well armed."

"Perhaps that is where Singh comes in," she said.

"You mean, in procuring arms?"

"I don't know, but it is possible."

"It's a dangerous game. The governor is getting tough, Ilka. He's threatening to hang a few of these rebels, as he calls them, as an example. I counseled him against it only today. But he seems determined."

For the first time that evening, Ilka dropped some of her reserve. Leighton could see her eyes beginning to smolder and feel her voice tightening.

"He is going to hang them, you say?" she flared up.

"That's what he threatens."

"Two can play at that kind of terror, I suppose," she said.

They had sat up another hour discussing the inhuman violence of the revolutions and counterrevolutions they had seen, the bloody ones of her youth in Budapest, the obscene purges in Berlin and Moscow, the massacre which Dollfuss wrought in Vienna and Franco, on a much larger scale, in Spain, and the slaughter they had seen once in Shanghai.

"At least you and I have a little perspective," Leighton smiled.

"But it never leaves you unconcerned — with tyranny, with man's inhumanity," Ilka added.

And then — quite ludicrously, it seemed to Leighton — they turned their thoughts as they went to bed to a quite trivial matter which had escaped his mind.

"Harold" — Ilka brought it up — "do you realize that two weeks from today is the Fourth of July?"

"My God, I had forgotten it was so soon," he said with genuine surprise. "It will be our last Fourth abroad, darling, do you realize that?" he added.

"I suppose you want to go through with our usual garden party?" Ilka said.

"Well, since it will be our last, I think I can take it. God, what bores they are!" Leighton exclaimed.

"We can make it our farewell party," Ilka said.

"Combine the two, that's fine, darling."

"Shall I go ahead with it, then?" she asked.

"By all means, darling. And if I can be of any help . . ."

"You never are," she smiled.

"It will probably rain," he said. "Then what do we do?"

"Herd the people in here, I suppose, like sardines."

"No, the monsoon came early this year. It should be pretty well spent by then."

"I hope so," she said. . . . "Oh God, how I hope so," she murmured to herself, and she was relieved that Harold, turning away for the moment, did not hear her or see the way her eyes must have lit up. A rain could be disastrous in more ways than he realized.

Chapter 4

THE RAINS let up the next afternoon and the firing from the direction of the docks below the consulate increased, reminding Leighton, as he left the office early to keep an appointment at home with Singh, of the battles of the war lords he had seen in China, where the troops of both sides abruptly ceased fighting when it rained, dropping their guns and raising their umbrellas. The struggle here, as indeed in recent years in the civil war in China, was more grim, and rain or shine Lord Branhope, as soon as he received reinforcements, was going to clear the rebels out of the docks and out of Pawancore City itself. It might be, though he himself doubted it, that if this happened and if the governor went ahead, as he had confided to Leighton that very morning he had decided, after much soul-searching, to do, with the hanging of a few rebel leaders under an old treason law, the Sikh and Hindu nationalists would be induced to abandon their armed resistance up in the hills and wait for the British to turn Pawancore over to them in a year or two or three. That would be the reasonable course, but in history, Leighton mused, there was little reason and in a revolution usually none at all, though there was undoubtedly a certain logic.

At any rate, he would be gone before the showdown, and once he was home, the troubles of Pawancore, the rights and wrongs of its awakened people, would soon fade in his mind as had those of so many other distraught lands and peoples where he had served. At this moment he was about to have a little showdown of his own and he wondered whether Singh would prove unduly difficult.

He really liked this complex and fiery young Sikh and he could readily understand why Isobel, in her youthful romanticism, had been bowled over by him. Thin, wiry, clean-shaven, with thick, black, shiny hair and almost too perfect features, Singh at first had reminded Leighton of a Hollywood hero. But there, in the outward appearance, he soon realized, the resemblance ended. He had been struck by the young man's warm, restless, intelligent eyes and the impression they gave of a high-strung, forceful nature that was kept in hand most of the time — at least until the trouble started — by an inner discipline.

It was difficult for the consul-general to imagine Singh as a Sikh at all. Unlike so many others, especially the older ones in Pawancore, who were orthodox, he declined to follow the five *kakkars* — the "five k's": the unshorn hair (*kesh*), the drawers reaching to the knees (*kachh*), the iron bangle (*kara*), the wooden comb (*khanga*), and the iron-handled knife (*kirpan*) around which the hair — and often the beard too — was rolled. Nor would Singh be seen in a turban.

Though he scorned his brethren who went off nearly every year on a holy pilgrimage to the great Sikh shrine of the Golden Temple at Amritsar in northern India, he apparently adhered to the Sikh religion. At least he had often spoken eloquently to Leighton of how it had reformed for its followers a decadent Brahmanical Hinduism, above all abolishing the obscene caste system. Indeed, the Guru Nanak, he said, who had founded Sikhism and who was a contemporary of Martin Luther, another religious reformer, had preached not only against caste but against the use of religious vestments, idolatry, ostentatious prayer and penance and even against pilgrimages.

"The Sikhs," Singh had also emphasized to him once, "are not a race but a brotherhood." It had been, in India, a fighting brotherhood, a sort of military as well as religious order, waging war first against the ruling Moslems and then the ruling British, and Leighton wondered whether this tradition had not had a special appeal to Singh — particularly in recent years after he returned home and became a dedicated man in the cause of national independence.

He had studied law in England, wore English-tailored clothes despite their unpopularity in Pawancore, and spoke English with somewhat of an Oxford accent modified by the clipped modulation of his native Sikh tongue. In the ten years or so since his return he had built up a fabulous law practice in the capital, becoming, Leighton would say, not only the most brilliant trial lawyer in the country but a most able and astute legal counselor on business and trade. Often, when some of Leighton's American businessmen were stymied by government regulations in their operations here, he had got Singh to help them out.

Leighton found Singh already in the living room conversing with Isobel.

"I was very sorry, sir, to hear your news," Singh said after they had exchanged greetings. "Your departure will be a loss not only to me personally but, believe me, to the people of this country."

Leighton was quite touched by this unexpected tribute. He had scarcely been aware that the people here even knew of his sympathy for them and their aspirations. Although he had made no secret of it, he had had to be, as the American consul-general, delicately diplomatic about it in his rare public utterances.

"I appreciate your sentiments, Singh," he replied. "One of the things that makes my going pleasant is the realization that the people of Pawancore are about to achieve their goal of independence."

"You think so, sir?" Singh thrust at him sharply.

"I am sure the British are planning to get out as soon

as they can — provided," and now he shook a finger good-naturedly at the young man, "provided the extremists in your Nationalist Party don't upset the timetable."

"It is difficult to keep the people in check," Singh said quietly.

"Some of you aren't trying very hard," Leighton said, half tauntingly and smiling knowingly. He wanted Singh to know that he was far from innocent about him.

"I do what I can," Singh said, breaking into a slight grin that partially exposed his fine, shining white teeth. "But I do not control the nationalist movement."

"You're certainly a major influence in it, Singh," Leighton persisted.

"Sometimes, perhaps." His face relaxed into a smile. "Only the other day, it is true, I found I had influence with some of our wild ones who wanted to set a little time bomb in the trunk of the American consul-general's Cadillac."

"Singh!" Isobel cried.

So the man was admitting his connection with the terrorists, Leighton thought quickly, but he joined Singh in a chuckle. "Why did they want to get me?"

"To raise a little hell . . . provoke complications . . . keep our own people in the proper stew . . . and, above all, embarrass the British."

"And more than embarrass me, eh?" Leighton chided him.

"Considerably more," Singh laughed. His face, Harold noticed, could change moods in a flash. "Seriously, sir, you need have no worry. As I said, we consider you our friend."

"I appreciate it," Leighton said lightly. It was about time now, he thought, to come to the point of the meeting. He watched Singh gracefully light Isobel's cigarette with his gold lighter and then his own — like most high-strung men he was an inveterate cigarette smoker. Leighton took advantage of the pause to fill his pipe and light it.

"Singh," he began, clearing his voice between puffs, "uh . . . there's something rather personal I wanted to mention to you . . ." He hesitated and glanced at his daughter. "Isobel, would you like to leave us alone for a moment?"

"On the contrary," she said tartly — "since I believe it concerns me."

"Very well," her father said — somewhat grimly, she thought. He turned to Singh. "This is rather a delicate matter, you understand. Perhaps with our going the problem resolves itself. Nevertheless . . ." He hesitated again, but Singh showed no signs of impatience, gazing at the older man with obvious good humor. "Singh, I think you realize that we Americans have no racial prejudices. We believe all men are equal regardless of color. We say so in our Constitution."

"I know you say so, sir," Singh said quietly, though

with a sparkle in his eye that Isobel loved. "But even we backward natives of Asia have heard, vaguely, of your South."

"I didn't say we had achieved perfection at home." Leighton raised his voice. "But we're making progress. The Negro is immensely better off today than he was a generation ago."

"I am happy to hear it, sir," Singh said.

"Now . . . uh . . ."

"Why don't you get to the point, Father?" Isobel broke in.

"Well, the point is . . . I think you will agree with me, Singh, that there are certain disadvantages in people of widely divergent . . . uh . . . backgrounds . . . marrying."

"I agree," Singh said, turning in time to catch Isobel's frown.

"I'm glad to hear you say that," Leighton said. "Singh, to come to the real point — what, may I ask, are your intentions toward my daughter?"

The young man looked straight at him with a twinkle in his eyes which reassured Leighton before a word was uttered. "Honorable, I assure you, sir."

"Specifically, I mean."

"I suppose you can say," Singh said, glancing good-naturedly at Isobel, "that we're genuinely good friends." He turned again toward Leighton. "I shall certainly be sorry, when you go, to be deprived of the occasional company which Isobel has so generously granted me."

A load slipped off the consul-general's mind. The whole affair, then, had been a fancy of a teen-ager's imagination. Ilka was right. Leighton glanced at his daughter. She was glaring at her friend, tears forming in her eyes. Leighton had intended to ask her once more to leave as soon as he had cleared up what concerned her. With Singh in such an apparently frank and genial mood it would be the best possible moment, perhaps the only one that remained, to extract from him some hint about Ilka. His worries about this Sikh revolutionary making off with his daughter had proved groundless. Probably the governor's suspicions regarding him and Ilka were equally baseless. Why — the thought passed swiftly through his mind — Singh was much less of a fanatic than he had been imagining all along. He had behaved with perfect reasonableness and restraint. He had been the quietest of the three of them throughout this painful business. To be sure, he had revealed — quite innocently — his connection with, indeed his authority over, the terrorists. But it looked to Leighton as if this might be the authority of the Nationalist Supreme Council, of which the young man was a member. The Council, probably, had delegated to Singh the job of keeping the terrorists in check.

If this were so, old Branhope's suppositions were completely off the track and to prod Singh about them, in regard to Ilka, might show Leighton up as a suspicious old fool. At any rate, he could not even approach the matter in Isobel's hearing and he had not the heart now to ask her to leave. She was sobbing, quietly but unrestrainedly, and the sight of her misery hurt him deeply. He went over to try to comfort her.

"I'll be all right in a minute," she murmured, wiping her eyes with her crumpled handkerchief. "It's just that . . ." But she did not finish the sentence.

Leighton took Singh's arm and moved with him toward the door. He would leave the two of them alone to seek what accommodation and understanding they could. Whatever had been the young man's motives, Isobel had completely misunderstood them. But he was mature enough and decent enough to let her down with tenderness and compassion.

"Singh," the consul-general said, clasping the other's hand firmly. "I'm glad we've had this opportunity to set matters straight. Isobel is very young. And I didn't want anything foolish to happen on the eve of our departure. I feel, from what you have said, that I can put the fullest trust in you in this regard."

"I assure you, you can, sir."

"But, Father." Isobel had obviously overheard them. "I —"

"I'm sorry, Isobel, but I have to go," Leighton called over to her. The matter had been settled; to prolong the talk would only aggravate her sense of injury. A child's

[56]

romantic world had come tumbling down on her, Leighton realized, and there was nothing he could do at the moment to help her bear the shock. Singh might help; however unintentionally, he had certainly misled her. He turned to Singh.

"You must excuse me." He shook Singh's hand warmly. "And by the way, you will be coming to our farewell garden party, I hope."

"When is that, sir?"

"On the Fourth."

"I shall certainly try to."

Leighton went out, mounting rapidly the steps to the bedroom, where he hoped he would find Ilka. She would be relieved to hear of his little triumph.

Singh walked slowly back to the divan and sat down at Isobel's side. For several minutes there was a silence, broken now and then by her effort to stifle a sob. When she finally gained control of herself and had wiped her eyes dry, she looked up to find Singh buried in thought, leaning forward, his chin resting on the palms of his hands, both elbows planted on his knees, his eyes fixed on the floor.

"How could you be so cowardly?" she said at last.

"Was I cowardly?" he said, not looking up.

"Yes, you were — giving in to Father without a word and denying everything there has been between us."

"We have to face the truth — and the facts of life," he said, turning toward her.

"The truth is I love you. And I am not leaving you, Singh."

"I appreciate your feelings," he said and the steely tone of his meager words shook her with sudden panic. "But let's face it, Isobel: in the end you will go home with your parents."

"I will not," she answered defiantly. "I am eighteen, and my own boss. I shall do what I want — and what you want."

"You Americans are wonderful!" Singh exclaimed, his eyes coming to life. "If our women had one ounce of your fierce spirit — to be free, to be independent — we wouldn't be groveling today in our slavery. Our women keep us back."

"I thought you did a little groveling yourself before my father just now," Isobel said. She started to grin, a little tauntingly.

"I did?" He did not seem to care. She noted with sinking heart the hollowness in his tone, the vacant look in his eyes.

"Telling him we were just good friends!" She tried to say it buoyantly and she tried to smile.

"Aren't we good friends?" he said, and she felt his chilling words cutting into her like pieces of jagged ice. And as if that were not cruel enough, his thoughts, she saw, seemed to be turning far away, beyond her reach

— she could divine it from his eyes. This was utter, final defeat — or was it? Desperately she tried a new tack.

"You mustn't take Father too seriously, Singh," she said, striving to sound lighthearted.

"He's a very fine man. I respect him."

"Of course he is. He's a dear. I love him. But like all fathers, I suppose, he doesn't quite realize that a daughter, when she gets to be eighteen, has her own life to lead."

She looked at Singh for a response, for words which might restore the ruin of her hopes — it was not too late. But he said nothing. Staring at the floor, he seemed to be more than ever lost in his thoughts. She lit her own cigarette and puffed it nervously waiting for him to speak. She smoked it down to the end before he stirred. Then he turned on her abruptly.

"Is your mother here?"

It was as if he had hit her with his fist. "I think so," she managed to say . . . "Why?"

"I would like to speak to her." He seemed to be staring through her with his piercing eyes. "Alone!"

"Oh . . . I see . . ." Perhaps she had misunderstood him. Her face brightened. "You don't have to convince Mother, my dear. She wants us to do" — she hesitated, but her eyes were lighting up — "whatever we think best."

"Could you call her?"

"Why, of course, Singh."

Torn between the suddenly renewed hope and the anguish of uncertainty which told her she might be merely desperately clutching at a straw, she got up slowly, and overcoming a momentary dizziness, made her way out of the room.

Chapter 5

Iʟᴋᴀ ᴡᴀs ʟʏɪɴɢ on her bed in a white silk dressing gown reading a mystery novel when her husband came in. Despite the oppressive heat of the late afternoon, when the winds and even the breezes often died away, she looked cool and comfortable, he thought. She glanced up as he came over to her side, and from the expression on his face she knew what had happened downstairs. Harold might hide his disappointments and defeats and even the worst of his worries — the discipline of a diplomat required it; but his little triumphs broke through his honest, sensitive face.

"Did you break it up?" she asked, taking a cigarette and waiting for him to light it. She would not deprive him of the pleasure of telling what was written all over his countenance.

"There wasn't much to break up, my dear," he said, with a sort of chuckle — "at least on Singh's side."

"Yes?"

"You were quite right, darling," he said, sitting down on the edge of the bed beside her. "Singh never had the slightest intention of seriously courting Isobel. He made that quite clear."

"There was nothing to worry about, then, after all," she smiled.

"No. You were right. And I was a bit of a fool, I'm afraid."

"Still, Isobel took it seriously, didn't she? I can't quite forgive Singh for allowing her to. He is old enough to know better."

"I honestly don't think he tried to mislead her," Leighton said. "It was just that Isobel is so young and so susceptible."

"Did she take it badly, poor thing?" Ilka asked.

"She was naturally terribly hurt. It was a case of the roof tumbling down on her. She sobbed and broke down — I could hardly stand it."

"How did Singh behave?" Ilka asked.

"Splendidly. I shall have to take back a lot of things I said and thought about him. He was completely open and aboveboard. And the calmest person in the room."

"Has he gone?"

"No. I left him to bind her wounds. He can do that better than I. As you say, he bears a certain responsibility. He owes it to her."

"Yes."

Leighton got up from the bed. "To think that I so misjudged the whole thing," he laughed, as if to himself.

"A mother," she smiled — "despite what the Freudians say — is sometimes closer to her daughter than the father."

"Yes, you've always been closer to Isobel than I. But isn't it natural, Ilka? She is at home most of the time with you. I'm away most of the time at the office. You can't help but know her better."

He paused, struck by a sudden thought. "The amazing thing, Ilka, is that you knew young Singh better than I. You were absolutely right about him all along."

"A woman's instinct, perhaps," she smiled.

"Yes, I suppose," he said. Did she suspect the hidden meaning in his remark? He meant the compliment sincerely but there was also a challenge in it which he hoped might stir some reaction in her face. But there was not the slightest change in her expression. Would he never know the thoughts that went on behind that beautiful but sphinxlike face! Or perhaps this time there were no secret thoughts, perhaps no grounds for them. Perhaps — indeed probably — she knew Singh no better than would be natural for the mother of a young girl he came to see occasionally and for the wife of an American official who not infrequently had the young man in for highballs or dinner.

At any rate there was no time to pursue the matter now, despite the opening he had tried to make. One day soon he would certainly summon the courage to tell Ilka what was on his mind, however foolish and absurd it might be. He would have to, for the sake of his peace of mind. At the moment, however, he must dress and hurry off to dinner at the Government House. Branhope was having another of his stag evenings while Lady Branhope was off in England on holiday. Leighton wished he did not have to leave Ilka and Isobel alone this evening. Bob Snow was going to the dinner too. Ordinarily on such occasions Bob would stay home and keep them company — good company too, for both of them dearly loved him.

Leighton glanced at his watch. "I have to dress and get off to Government House," he said, leaning forward to kiss her on her forehead. She cupped her hands behind his neck and pulled his head down gently and held his lips to hers.

"I worry when you go out alone in the evening," she said softly. "It seemed to me a few minutes ago that the firing was getting awfully near."

"It's the breeze," he said, "blowing up from the bay. It makes the rumpus down by the docks sound closer than it is. There's nothing to worry about, darling. Branhope has sealed the thing off."

"But they infiltrate at night down from the hills, don't they?" she asked.

"Not enough of them to matter. Besides, Ilka, I have Bob as protection tonight."

"Is Bob going too?"

"Yes. And that leaves you and Isobel alone, which I

don't much like, especially after what has just happened."

"We shall be all right," Ilka said.

"Isobel will probably be quite difficult," he suggested.

"I can cope with her, I think," she smiled.

"I know you can, darling." He matched her smile.
He kissed her again and stood up.

"Will you remember to remind the governor," Ilka
said, her hand clinging to his, "of our party on the
Fourth? Tell him it will be our farewell."

"He would come anyway." The thought brought a
smile to Leighton's face. "The British always help us
celebrate the Fourth, you know."

Ilka still held his hand. "I'm surprised at Bob Snow,"
she said.

"Why, darling?"

"Going to Government House with you. He's so fu-
rious at the old man — because of the hangings."

"Branhope hasn't hanged anyone yet, Ilka," Leighton
said.

"But you've been telling me he was threatening to,"
Ilka said, and now her deep voice was almost shrill, and
rasping, as it became lately, he noticed, whenever she
talked of Branhope.

"As a matter of fact . . ." Leighton said, and then
hesitated, a frown darkening his face.

"Yes?" Ilka said sharply.

[65]

". . . He told me this morning he had made up his mind to go ahead with the thing . . . under some old treason law."

"That's definite?" Ilka asked, and Leighton was surprised to see her — she who was always so completely in control of herself — struggling fiercely to keep herself in check.

"That was my impression," Leighton replied.

"I wonder . . ." Ilka said, and now, he saw, she had mastered her nerves, for she spoke in an even, low tone and her eyes seemed distant. ". . . I wonder . . . if he will get away with it."

"I'm doing my best, Ilka, believe me," he said earnestly, "to dissuade him. I shall hammer away at him again this evening."

"He's a callous old tyrant," Ilka said heatedly. "He won't listen. What are the lives of a few brown-skinned natives to His Lordship? Nothing!"

Ilka had just doffed her dressing gown after a parting word with Leighton and Snow, and was debating in her mind what would be coolest to put on for the evening, which promised to be one of the most sweltering of the summer, when Isobel came in, her eyes bleary and reddened, her face so crestfallen, so stricken with distress, that her mother, who had never seen her quite like this before, felt a lump grow suddenly in her heart.

"Singh wants to see you, Mother," Isobel blurted out. "Alone, he says. He's in the living room."

Ilka took her in her arms and held her, feeling the convulsions that ran through Isobel's back. "Harold has just told me," she said quietly. "I'm sorry."

Isobel broke away. "Father was horrible. You can't imagine it, Mother. He talked Singh out of everything. It was . . . criminal," she said, beginning to sob again.

Ilka smothered her in her arms again, like a baby. "I know how you feel," she said, patting her shoulders.

Isobel looked up, the plea loud in her eyes that eagerly sought her mother's. "You can still save us, Mother! Will you try? Will you speak to him!"

"Your father has just left."

"With Singh, I mean. He was so cowardly. But I know he didn't mean to be. It was just that Father so impressed him. He is downstairs now. He wants to speak to you. Oh, Mother!" she cried. "You can help. You understand us. Will you tell Singh — tell him what you really feel about us!"

"I'll talk to him," Ilka said.

She found Singh, a cigarette dangling from his lips, pacing the floor nervously. "Won't you sit down?" She smiled slightly, taking a seat on the divan and bidding him with a gesture of her finger to sit down beside her. She took a cigarette from the table and turned for him

[67]

to light it, murmuring a "Thank you," and then sat silently for a moment exhaling the smoke through her nostrils and gazing at the wall opposite. She was conscious of his eyes peering at her restlessly, those eyes which Harold once had said were like her own, jet-black and brooding, but she knew that, impatient as he was, he would wait for her to say the first words.

She flicked the ashes of her half-burnt cigarette on the ash tray on the table at her side and then turned to the man and met his eyes.

"Why did you do it, Singh?"

"What?"

"Deceive her so long. She's a sweet, innocent child. You could see that."

"I am very fond of Isobel," Singh said. "You know that."

"You should not have deluded her then. It was not necessary."

Singh sat back slightly, his eyes flashing at her. But a smile formed on his lips too.

"You know it was necessary," he said, "to cover up. And protect you."

"You don't have to worry about me."

"But I do," he said.

Again they fell into a silence, but this time their eyes continued to meet as if each were trying to size up for the last time the mettle of the other. Ilka finally broke the silence.

"Are you going ahead?" she asked in a matter-of-fact tone.

Singh glanced back at the door. "Is Mr. Leighton upstairs?"

"No. He left. For Government House. With Bob Snow."

"Good," Singh said. "We can talk, then . . . Yes, we're going ahead."

"It's not just talk this time?"

"How could it be?" Singh said. "It has become a question of our getting him before he gets us."

"Harold told me. He is going ahead with the hangings — under some old treason law. This is the first chance I've had to tell you."

"We found out. I . . ." Singh broke into a smile. "I am on the list myself."

"No!"

"Why not?" It is a nervous smile, Ilka thought, but a brave one. "The old duffer suspects what I am up to," Singh said. "We have a few traitors of our own, you know. It is inevitable."

"Isn't it more important," Ilka said, "for you to concentrate on your main job?" She could never, it suddenly flashed on her, face the reality of Singh dead, hanged.

"What job?"

"Running arms."

"I've got that nicely organized," he replied. "A child can handle it now."

"I hate the killing, Singh," she said.

"They're killing plenty of us. And now, as you say, the hangings."

"I know." For some days she had doubted that this sleek and handsome young man who got so much pleasure out of life, who extracted so much meaning from it, had the necessary resolve, of granite, to go through with what had been burning their thoughts, and now she felt doubts of her own arising. Was Singh beginning to suspect them? He faced her with his intense eyes.

"We have been waiting on you," he said.

"For what?"

"The date."

"We only decided on it last night," she said.

"I know. He just told me. The Fourth — July Fourth, he said." Singh spoke quickly.

"He had forgotten. I had to remind him."

"It's definite? We can count on it?"

"Yes."

"That gives us thirteen days," Singh said.

"Is it enough?"

"It will have to be enough," Singh said, determinedly.

"What if it rains?" Ilka put the question that had stuck in her mind since the evening before.

"It won't. It can't. The monsoon will be over," Singh said, but she could see the suggestion made him uneasy.

"You can never tell about a monsoon, can you?"

[70]

"I am sure it will be spent," Singh said. "It came early this year."

"It would be impossible if it rained, wouldn't it?" Ilka said.

"Yes," Singh said, frowning.

"We would have to herd everyone inside. There would be no room. Too many people. You couldn't do it, could you?" she asked anxiously.

"No," he said firmly. "It would be out of the question."

"It was so easy — those other things," Ilka said.

"Burning up Groves's oil tank and dynamiting Kelly's warehouse, you mean?" Singh smiled.

"Yes. They went off so easily, didn't they?"

"There was no problem of killing anyone — perhaps that's why," Singh said. "This time it's different. We don't want any innocent people hurt — white or brown."

"Have you any idea how you are going to do it?" Ilka asked, and the question, which she knew could no longer be put off, and which she herself must finally squarely face, frightened her.

"I've been thinking of it," Singh said. "We will work it out, you and I. It is largely a matter, as I see it now, of your getting the old man aside, alone, so I can get at him."

Ilka felt suddenly too faint to reply.

"One final thing," she heard Singh say. "We can be absolutely certain that he will be here?"

[71]

"He has never failed us yet on the Fourth," she found the strength to say. "I think you can count on it, Singh."

For how long Ilka sat there rigidly after Singh left, smoking one cigarette after the other, she did not know. She was aware only of struggling, as if in a nightmare, to claw her way back to reality, to the other part of her being that was rooted to the earth, to her existence as the wife of a decent and gifted man whom she still loved and as the mother of a child who was dear to her, to the role she had played so long as the wife of an American official, a helpmate in his difficult job in strange lands such as this, as presider over his household, a sharer in his fate, whatever it had been or would be.

And then Isobel came in, her face alight with hope.

"Oh, Mother! What did you say! What did he say! Please tell me!"

Ilka could only take her in her arms, lay her head on her own quivering shoulder and mumble soothing words that were deceiving by their very meaninglessness and which, as she uttered them, stabbed at her throbbing heart.

Chapter 6

GRADUALLY over the last year or so Singh had come to understand what had turned Ilka Leighton toward him and him toward her.

It was not really a matter of love. He had been attracted, as he knew other men had been, by her beauty and even more by her strange magnetism and the inscrutable nature of her being, and like so many others — like her husband, like Robert Snow — he had soon begun to worship her. Love? In the deep and secret recesses of his soul there had surged a passion and a longing he had never felt for any other woman. But he had stifled them. She had never given him much reason to believe that she reciprocated them, though he was sure that she liked and admired him. What love she had for a man, as a man, as a lover, she gave to her husband, but even if that had not been the case, even if she had somehow come to share the suppressed feelings he had for her, his sense of honor, his respect and affection for Harold Leighton, would have prevented the flowering of a folly.

But not only that. Love and its passions, its transports and its torments, he knew, would have thrown them off the narrow and dangerous track that they began to follow together, distracting and weakening his own resolve to plunge ahead to the end of it in a cause that in the last year or two had become infinitely more important to him than one's love or one's life. By an inner discipline he had forced himself to keep this crystal-clear in his mind — above all other considerations — on two or three occasions when he himself weakened and when he felt that she was weakening and that the passion of love might flame up and envelop them.

What fundamentally had drawn them together, Singh saw, was the nature of their experience of life and of their reaction to it.

Despite his lifetime service abroad and his intelligence and perceptiveness and learning, Harold Leighton, it became clear to Singh, was bound to have quite different concepts than theirs. Being a native-born American and an American official who had served his country loyally and with sympathetic understanding, Leighton could never have quite the uncertainties, the reservations, the skepticism regarding the ordering of mankind which Ilka — and he himself — had come to have.

Though he had never even visited the United States, Singh thought he knew something about it. He had studied it in all the courses he could find in the universities in England and had gone out of his way both there and here in Pawancore to cultivate Americans. He devoured American books and subscribed to the *New York Times* and *Time* magazine. He had been fascinated since his early school days by American history, by the saga of the conquest of a continent, by the story of the making of a new giant among the nations and, later, of its gradual awakening to its power and position in the world. He admired the rough practice of American democracy, though he thought he was not blind to its faults — if he had his way he would adopt it, by and large, for Pawancore as soon as his country should be free. He liked the spirit of freedom he found in most Americans he met and in so much American writing. He was enthusiastic about America's technical genius — Pawancore and indeed all of Asia would never be truly free until they discovered it, or at least tried to emulate it, as Japan had done.

And he found Americans as a people, as a nation, to be the most generous in their dealings with the outside world of perhaps any in all history. They sought no colonies and had rapidly shed those few which, by an accident of war, they had stumbled upon. They were shelling out billions to help their allies — and even their late enemies — recover from the recent war. What other great country had ever done such a thing? Not England, not France, not Germany, not Russia, not Japan. True, the accounts he read sometimes, and the novels, about the inhumanity of white Americans toward black Americans depressed him. But, as Leighton had often emphasized, even that situation was improving and it had to be looked at — though not justified — in the perspective of what was going on in South Africa, where the Negroes were treated worse than cattle, and what had gone on in nearby India, from which his ancestors had come, and where for centuries, until very recently, forty or fifty million so-called untouchables had been rigorously excluded through sheer superstition from the human family.

But much as he admired America, Singh knew that it had made such men as Harold Leighton and Robert Agate Snow — even though he realized that they were far from being "typical" Americans; he would call them the best of Americans — had made them largely impervious to certain challenges of the uneasy times which in the end had brought Ilka Leighton and himself so close because they felt they could not dodge or ignore them.

The stability of life in the United States for nearly a century — since 1865, when the Civil War ended — and the resulting material prosperity and the easy victories in wars abroad which had scarcely touched the bulk of the people, who remained at home far from the battlefields and the bombings, had made the Americans, it seemed to Singh, the most conservative people on the planet, causing them to replace in this regard the British, who, at home at least, were losing their conservatism because they were losing their wealth and their self-confidence based on world supremacy, sovereignty over half the globe, mastery of the seas and all the fabulous profits in monies and goods which this unique position had given them for two centuries.

The Americans had become so conservative, Singh often put it to Leighton, that their two political parties, unlike those of most other countries in the West, had no essential differences, both being financed and dominated by businessmen. Moreover, the businessman's narrow view of life so permeated the country through control of mass communications that it had succeeded in giving Americans — whether they were aware of it or not, and perhaps most were not — a one-sided version, and a highly superficial one at that, of the complexities and the tragedy of man's life on earth.

It was natural, Singh conceded, for the Americans to have a deep instinct to preserve intact, unchanged, what seemed good to them, or what they were told through the newspapers, the magazines, the cinema, the radio, T.V. (and from many a pulpit and schoolmaster's desk) was good for them. The Americans had concocted the most formidable collection of mechanical gadgets the world had ever seen. And while Singh did not take the usual Asian view, the one that the great Gandhi had preached, that these contraptions were bad in themselves — indeed he saw that they could be beneficial too for his own people, if they could ever afford them, relieving them of some of the incredible drudgery of their mean and starving lives — he felt appalled that the Americans apparently had accepted them not as a means to liberate individuals for a deeper, more meaningful, more cultivated and more spiritual life but as an end of living itself. Was that not the dismal conclusion one had to draw from reading the slick advertisements in the American magazines? Or even the articles, editorials and stories sandwiched in between the ads?

But Singh kept coming back to his main point — that life for Americans, basking in their individual freedom and national independence, had gone on tranquilly for nearly a hundred years. Even the depression, which had hit the United States hardest of all countries, had not driven Americans to any serious questioning of their economic-social system. No socialist or labor party had risen from the debris as in England and Scandinavia and other countries.

This tranquillity, this freedom, this stability, had not been given in this century to many other peoples, not to the Hungarians, for example, from whom Ilka had come, and not to Singh's fellow Asians.

Ilka had unfolded to him the story of her own university days in Budapest just after the 1914-1918 war, when first the red terror and then the white had driven her not only from the academic halls, depriving her of a formal higher education, but from her native land at the very moment when the overthrow of the Hapsburgs had promised Hungarians for the first time complete political independence and real democracy.

Striving in Vienna to recover from the shock, she had seen that after the war's holocaust and the revolutions and counterrevolutions and all the chaos there would be little repose for most Europeans in the years ahead. But she was twenty; she could make a fresh start in the only country left, aside perhaps from England and France, where there seemed to be stability, security and opportunity for an individual such as herself. She would emigrate to America. But the quotas were full; she might have to wait years for her turn. Perhaps, the idea had come to her, if she could get a job in the American legation or consulate-general, that might facilitate getting to the New World. She had wangled a job, thanks to her knowledge of English.

And then, she related to Singh, a stroke of good fortune had occurred. She had fallen in love with a man who could give her the stability and security she was seeking.

But was it that which she really wanted? She thought so. She had sought and found it with unexpected suddenness and ease, and in a man who more than reciprocated her love. Quickly married to Leighton, she had plunged into his life as a young diplomat and consular officer, succeeding more fully than she had expected, and much sooner, in pushing the jagged memories of the immediate past into the limbo of her consciousness.

The personal lives of millions of uprooted Europeans, of her own friends, of her own family — her father, a fine surgeon and, like most professional middle-class Hungarians, an ardent liberal-democrat, had committed suicide in prison and her mother had died from the shock — their lives had been shattered and few of those who continued to exist physically would ever be able to piece them together again. But she had been able to begin a new life, and she was happy.

"Way down, though, in the marrow of your bones, were you?" Singh had asked, and she had read in his face the hint of an accusation: that it must have been a false happiness because it was based on selfishness.

"I think I really was happy," she answered. "Undoubtedly there was a selfishness in it. But was it selfishness to devote yourself to a man you loved and admired, to make him an attractive home in one place after another, to help him in his work, to sustain him when the going was rough and he faltered?"

"That was unselfish," Singh said.

He thought he knew what the next part of her account would be. For what had happened to her, he was sure, was similar to an awakening which had occurred in him. There had come the moment that proved to be the watershed of his life when the flashing of some great light within transformed the contemplative man into the man of action, the *talker* into the *doer*.

He had often told her how it had happened. He had

not been much concerned with the aspirations of his fellow Sikhs and Hindus when he returned from England to begin the practice of law. British rule was something you accepted, like your religion, however much you questioned it. He did not particularly like the English. In Pawancore, as at home, they were arrogant, insensitive to others, lacking in imagination. But they had a knack of governing well; they were at least honest, and, compared to Asians, efficient. After all, Singh liked to tell himself, they had replaced the medieval barbarism and corruption of Pawancore's Hindu emperor, whom they had deposed in the mid-seventeen-hundreds, with a relatively modern administration of some integrity. In fact, most of the corruption came from native Pawancorese, Sikh and Hindu politicians, who sought office under the British not so much to gain power — power was reserved for the Englishman — as to amass a fortune.

Singh himself at first, he explained to Ilka, had not been averse to working with the British rulers, for he had seen at once which was the easiest and quickest and perhaps the only way to achieve his ambition of becoming the biggest lawyer in the land. He had served on more than one occasion as special government prosecutor and for two years, after what he supposed was a fairly spectacular rise at the bar, as the ranking "native" official in the so-called Law Department.

"If I had stayed on in government" — he chuckled at

the very thought when he recounted this to Ilka — "I probably would have become, at thirty or so, a minister in the governor-general's cabinet. Actually, I left," he confessed to her, "not because of any strong nationalist feelings but, I am ashamed to say, because I knew I could make more money in private practice."

He had needed a lot of money those first years, he explained, to live the kind of Westernized life he had become familiar with, and liked, in London. The way he found most Sikhs and Hindus living when he returned revolted him; they seemed to wallow in filth. He had to have a sumptuous villa in the "diplomatic quarter" above Pawancore City, with half a dozen pink-tiled bathrooms, a bar, a cellar full of French wines, champagnes and brandies, and outside, in the front of the spacious lawn, a blue-tiled, kidney-shaped swimming pool right out of Hollywood. Servants of course were cheap, but it took money to supply himself with suits from Savile Row in London and a new car every year or two from America. And it took money to entertain lavishly so many Americans and French and English and other white-skinned foreigners.

"In short," he had said once to Ilka, "I became an utter fool, carried away by my own self-importance, impressed by my own eloquence at the bar, by money which came so easily, by fame as a lawyer, by the way your Europeans and Americans sought my counsel and my company. And all the time — and this now seems the most inexplicable of all — though I followed developments in England, in Europe and even in America — I was blind, I was completely oblivious, to what was going on beneath the surface here in Pawancore, not to mention in the rest of Asia."

Beneath the surface, and more and more as time went rapidly on, above the surface, out in the open, a great deal was going on, and finally Singh became aware of some of it. A number of the cases he took after resigning from the Law Department began to open his eyes. He found himself defending his fellow citizens against political charges, against accusations of "inciting, or attempting to incite, disaffection toward His Majesty's Government, established by law in Pawancore," as the words of an old statute he had never previously heard of put it, and it suddenly struck him, greatly to his astonishment, that despite all his forensic talents and what was more important, the justice of his pleas, the courts, dominated by bewigged English jurists as they were, were sending an increasing proportion of his clients to jail and with stiff terms.

At first, these sentences had merely hurt his pride as a defense lawyer. But as he probed into his cases and his experience of losing most of them grew, it dawned on him, he explained to Ilka, that the laws which the British had promulgated and were now enforcing so rigorously were merely crude instruments to prevent the people of Pawancore from obtaining in any measurable future that self-rule which the British government in London had promised them during the First World War, when the Allied fortunes of war were at a low ebb and the British needed troops from India and Pawancore to save their crumbling position in the Near East.

Most of the Sikhs and Hindus he initially defended were confused and, it seemed to him, mediocre men — starving journalists, unsuccessful lawyers, disappointed office-seekers — who had got out badly printed, wretchedly written pamphlets calling for the British to honor their word and get out. But a few of the men had impressed him not only by their unselfish devotion to what after all, Singh began to see, any self-respecting Asian wanted — national independence — but by their intelligence and their diligence in making clear how, on the whole, British rule had been an evil thing in Pawancore. It had drained the wealth of the land, they showed, off to England, leaving the great mass of the people — people whom Singh had scarcely ever seen or thought of — mired in sloth and poverty, wretched in their rags with disease and hunger. Worse, they argued, it had brought a spiritual death to the people of Pawancore — to seek the life of the spirit, to possess human dignity, men had to be free.

Singh listened, visited the countryside to see for himself, read books, pored over statistics and, above all, snatched time to reflect on what for him, blind as he had been, was a revelation. He became a nationalist; he joined the Pawancore Nationalist Party.

But it was, he emphasized to Mrs. Leighton, as a thinker, a talker. He studied and pondered; he spoke at public meetings; he wrote articles for some of the nationalist magazines; he gave over most of his law practice to defending political offenders. He took good care, however, not to risk going to jail himself. Knowing the law, he was able to circumvent it in his speeches and writing. He tried to convince himself, as he said to Ilka, that he was more valuable to the cause out of prison, where he could devote himself to defending the unjustly accused. The truth was that he had no stomach for the role of political martyr or for the stench of overcrowded British jails. He was still too fond of the civilized, Westernized life. He declined to don native dress, as most of the other Westernized nationalist leaders had done. So far as his outward existence went, it continued much as before — if not quite so luxurious, it was still very comfortable.

Inwardly, though, it was surely changing. In defending those charged with disaffection, Singh rarely won a case. The charge itself — "of inciting, or attempting to incite, disaffection toward His Majesty's Government" — was absurd. How could you create affection, or punish its absence or its opposite by law? If you didn't like a system or a government or a governor you ought to be free to say so. This was a fundamental human right, denied only by the totalitarians and the other tyrannnies. But Singh's arguments at the bar were of no avail. The judgments against those he represented and the severe sentences imposed upon them became almost automatic. This, however, no longer frustrated him. He began to see that it was all to the good. Men and women had to go to jail in order to set an example for the masses and kindle in them the flames of defiance and resistance to foreign rule. Sometimes when he addressed a mass meeting in the upcountry he was encouraged by the reaction. These ragged, hungry, illiterate people, looking more like skeletons than living beings, had been aroused. He found it increasingly easy to fire them.

But was that enough? Was it not necessary now to organize them and go over to more positive action? The prisons were full of patriots. But the British remained firmly in the saddle. True, they had again promised, during the recent war, that they would get out of Pawancore "at an early date." Apparently they were going to keep their word to get out of India, but this was because their position there was becoming untenable. Pawancore had no Gandhi or even a Nehru. Its Nationalist Party was but a diluted version of the all-powerful Indian National Congress which Gandhi had built up. It became obvious to Singh that the British were going to linger on as long as possible in Pawancore; indeed, if they gave up India presently, they would be tempted to hold on to Pawancore as one of their last bastions in Asia.

At the end of the war there had been negotiations with the governor-general. Singh himself had been named to the Supreme Council of the Nationalist Party and had taken part in them. It was plain that Lord Branhope was stalling. When the Council had demanded a specific date — within two years — for the termination of the British connection, Branhope had broken off negotiations and had warned that he would put down with armed force any resistance to "law and order." Over the objections of a number of the more timid members of the Council, Singh had taken the lead in insisting on a definite time limit. His strategy had failed. His bluff, as the governor-general termed it to his face at the final session of the talks, had been called. What next?

That was the moment, he told Ilka, that he reached the watershed of his life. He had been talking and arguing with his sharp lawyer's tongue for years. Now there had to be action. As Gandhi had so long preached in India, force had to be met by force. But though Gandhi had meant, and sincerely meant, nonviolent force, it seemed to Singh that there had been plenty of violence by the nationalists in India whom Gandhi could not control. Was that not what had led the British there, in the final analysis, to decide to capitulate? If so, was the course to be followed in Pawancore not obvious?

[87]

"Thus," Singh explained to Ilka, "I became, I suppose you could say, a doer. I helped persuade the Council that we must pass over to armed resistance. I threw myself into the job of procuring arms and training men to use them. We answered their armed force with some of our own. And more recently, when Branhope, in his desperateness, threatened to resort to outright terror, to his hangings, I convinced our people that two could play at that game. In fact, before he got us and strung us up, I decided, we must get him."

Chapter 7

THAT HAD BEEN the road, Singh told
Ilka, that he had traversed up to the present moment
of climax, but in between the telling of it, which went
on over the months in which they slowly came together,
he had listened to her continue the account of her trav-
els toward him.

It had not been easy for them to snatch moments
alone. For the most part they came to know each other
during the hours of general conversation in the company
of Harold and Isobel, when Singh would drop by after
dinner for a highball ostensibly to talk business with
Leighton and — as Isobel must have thought — to further his courtship with her, and would linger on to
ruminate with them about life and the world. As the
need to communicate in privacy grew they resorted to
various stratagems to achieve a few moments, now and
then, here and there, by themselves. If Singh were invited to tea he would arrive half an hour early — before
Leighton had returned from the office or Isobel from
her tennis and golf. The country club, Ilka thought,

might have provided a suitable rendezvous, but there was a strict color bar there and Singh had been too proud to fall in with her suggestion that he try to break it by applying for membership.

"Think of how miserable some of those old fogies would be," he had joked with her, "if they were no longer able to boast that no man of color had ever crossed the portals of the Pawancore Golf and Country Club!"

Sometimes they contrived to get apart from others at the numerous parties given by the consular set, and at the week-end gatherings around Singh's swimming pool there were further opportunities. More recently, throwing caution to the winds, Ilka had skipped an occasional afternoon bridge party and had driven to an unfrequented beach up the coast where Singh would be waiting and where they could sit in his car or hers and smoke and talk.

Despite the tantalizing reserve of this strange woman, Singh could not help thinking that under his prompting and gentle prodding — or was it more because of her natural reaction to all he had said and all that her eyes had been opened to out here? — she was baring more of herself, of one vital core of her inner life, than she had ever done before, even to her husband.

With Harold Leighton, she told him, she had found love and understanding and the satisfying of her craving to flee away from the hideous memories of her youth to a life that was sane, secure, orderly, decent. She would have followed Harold anywhere, but she was disappointed at first that since she was marrying an American they could not go off at once, and forever, across the wide ocean to America, where there would no longer be even a reminder of the helpless, tragic plight of so many of her fellow Europeans.

"If Harold had been a businessman," she mused one day to Singh, her dark eyes lighting up, "I would have gone to live, no doubt, in some comfortable, placid suburb of a great American city, and nothing much would have happened to me, I imagine, except inevitable decay."

"You would have been too restless to stay," Singh smiled.

"I would have conquered that," Ilka answered.

As it was, Leighton's work during the first years had taken them from one European capital or industrial city to another, and inevitably her thoughts and her energies were taken up mostly with the pleasant, busy life a young couple in the diplomatic and consular circles invariably led. Even though in many places, she said, masses of people were half starving in their hovels and, often, in revolt, or seething with revolt, or being put down bloodily because of revolt, life for the foreign diplomats and their families went on undisturbed by, and largely unmindful of, such conditions, revolving around gala dinners, cocktail parties, evenings of bridge and, during the long winters, gay, fancy costume balls.

It was not, she tried to explain to Singh, that she and Leighton were oblivious to what went on around them. It was part of his job to know, and he wrote long and graphic accounts of it for the State Department and usually discussed them with her at home. Often, after such discussions, they would share a dark moment of depression or a burning one of indignation. Sometimes, with Harold's encouragement, Ilka would plunge into a work of charity that gave her a feeling that she was doing some small thing to help alleviate the misery of at least a few human beings.

But always, for them, there was the escape, when evening came, to the gay social life which went on for the diplomats and for the native upper classes, and while Harold's existence remained centered in his work at the embassy or the consulate, her own became more and more rooted in the swirl of parties. It seemed to be the inevitable fate of a diplomat's wife.

In the beginning, she said, she did not mind it. In fact, to be truthful, she enjoyed it immensely, and all the more so because it seemed a just compensation for all the wretchedness of her life in Budapest just after the war. Even during that first war, and despite the hardships, the shortage of food and fuel and clothing, the absence at the front of so many young men, Budapest had retained a certain gaiety, and for a blossoming Hungarian girl in her teens there had been parties, balls, gypsy music, flirtations and even what seemed like romance.

"At heart," she remarked to Singh, "we Hungarians are a simple, primitive, lighthearted, fun-loving race. We like to sing, to dance, to drink heady wines, get dizzy over gypsy music, flirt and make love."

So in those first years, she said, she wined and danced a good deal and mastered bridge. "When I think of the hours, the thousands of hours," she mused, "I have whiled away at bridge, the principal pastime of all diplomatic sets no matter where, I am appalled!"

Singh could picture her, this dark and hauntingly beautiful woman, moving gracefully and enigmatically among the politically and socially elite of the postwar European capitals. She must have been the center of attraction in any gathering and she surely broke many hearts. She did not speak much of her life with Leighton — that was something which did not concern Singh, or any other person — but it was not difficult for Singh to feel from what she implied that it had been a rich and full life founded on a deep and enduring love. Sometimes she had joked with him, as he had heard her joke with Snow, about how fickle and flirtatious Hungarian women were. But even in her younger days, when her beauty must have been breathless and when men flocked around her adoringly and hungrily and temptingly, she must have kept them, Singh was sure, at a tantalizing distance, declining to indulge even in an innocent coquetry because such a pose was foreign to her nature and, in any case, would not have been necessary. Leighton in those earlier days must have been, Singh could see too, an attractive partner for so lovely and fascinating a woman, with his sensitive face, his youthful but manly manner, his genial charm, his quick intelligence. They would have been happy and harmonious together and sufficient to themselves anywhere under any circumstances, however overwhelming.

In the gay and superficial social world they had been thrust into by the nature of his employment there were, of course, certain opportunities, Ilka tried to explain to Singh, for a diplomat's wife. If she kept her ears open, she picked up pieces of gossip and even of information that were useful to Harold in his work. She was able to size up the men — and sometimes the women — who had the power in the country, and which ones were on the point of losing it or gaining it and for what purposes — and this too was useful to her husband and his office. In the weird and fickle universe of politics and diplomacy one acquired most acquaintanceships and "contacts" amid the swirl of social goings-on. A foreign minister or a prime minister, for that matter, talked more freely over cigars and liqueur, after a good dinner tempered by champagne and the company of beautiful women elegantly gowned, than was likely in the austere office of a chancellery.

In time, though, she and Leighton began to be bored

with the life; it became gradually more of a duty than a pleasure. Harold gave an increasing amount of his spare time to study; to learning languages and reading history. And she commenced to give more thought, she said, to what was going on all around her.

There slowly began an awakening, she told Singh, that was akin to his. Tyranny and its abominations, she found, were not confined to her native Hungary. Like most of her fellow students at the University of Budapest, she had been stirred by the flaming promises of Woodrow Wilson that the Allies were fighting the war to make the world safe for democracy. But she found little democracy in the countries they worked and lived in. After Prague, they had been sent to Riga in Latvia, where the American legation served as a listening post for Soviet Russia, with which the United States at that time did not have diplomatic relations. Exaggerated and secondhand though the reports were that came in from the Soviet Union to the Riga legation, there could be no denying that not only was there no democracy, no political freedom, in Russia but that Lenin, a ruthless genius, had succeeded in setting up a tyranny that was even more crushing than that of the czars, if only because it was more thorough and efficient. The Soviet dictator was exterminating not only the upper classes which had opposed him but thousands of the very men who had helped him make the revolution, the Mensheviks and the Social Revolutionaries. It was while at

Riga that they learned of the frightful massacre of the Social Revolutionary sailors at Kronstadt — an act of savagery, she and Leighton thought, from which even Ivan the Terrible or Peter the Great might have shrunk. Later, when the United States resumed diplomatic relations with Russia and the Leightons were sent to Moscow, she had seen Stalin, the worthy successor to Lenin, turn on the very leaders of his own Bolshevik party, men who had played greater roles in the October Revolution than he, and send them, after rigged trials which Ilka herself attended, one after the other, to slaughter before a firing squad. Ilka had become numbed by the experience of seeing the lives of a great and attractive people suffocated, when they were not arbitrarily snuffed out, by a gang of brutal tyrants.

"As chance had it," she told Singh one day, "we went next to Berlin. Hitler's was another kind of tyranny — my education was broadening, you see. The oppression in Germany was not so harsh, not so primitive, as we had seen in Russia. But in one way, at least, it was worse."

"Worse?" Singh asked.

"Yes, because it was accepted and indeed supported by the overwhelming majority of Germans. They participated enthusiastically — you had to see it, Singh, to believe it — in giving up their freedom to a despot. There were exceptions, of course. There were Germans, a few, who valued liberty and decency. At the embassy we got to know quite a number of them. We helped some escape to America. But most were carted off to concentration camps. The Jews among them, of course, never came back."

That reminded Ilka of another difference between Moscow and Berlin.

"In Russia, the Bolsheviks exterminated their foes and their followers out of a medieval fear for their own security as top dogs. With Stalin this ultimately became a mania. But the Nazis, it has always seemed to me, massacred millions of Jews out of sheer sadism, sheer savagery. The Jews were never a threat to Hitler's rule and he knew it."

"What an education you were getting!" Singh said. "It makes mine seem pale in comparison."

"Of course," Ilka told him, "there were intervals when we were stationed in normal countries. Washington, London, Paris, Stockholm, for example. They enabled you to regain your senses, restore your feelings of balance. But living in them briefly also served, by its very contrasts, to sharpen and deepen your resentment, your sense of outrage, at what you had seen in these other places. Life didn't have to be such a degradation. History — all the injustices of the past — may have contributed to it. But in the end it was human beings who, out of utter depravity, took the liberties and the lives of these peoples."

Finally, the Leightons had had a brief sojourn in

Spain toward the end of the civil war. There had been frightful butcheries on both sides, she conceded, but it was Franco who — thanks to German and Italian Nazi-Fascist help — emerged as one more autocrat of the times, crushing the spirit and the aspirations of one of the most decent and courageous peoples she had ever known.

Asia, Ilka said, had been difficult for her, at first, to understand. The situation of the people was quite different from that in Europe. Though it was no consolation to the oppressed, at least most of the oppressing in Europe was done by one's own fellow countrymen. In most of Asia it was carried out by foreigners on behalf of foreign lands. The mass of the people didn't seem to mind. Or at least, that was her impression before the second war, when she and Leighton had come out on their first assignment in the Orient. The teeming millions seemed to her to wallow in their filth and ignorance under the Europeans as they had before under their own native rulers. There had been no change — for them. How could they aspire to something better since, over the centuries and the generations, they had never experienced it?

"No man or woman, even Asian," Singh had answered, "was ever content to be hungry. He aspires, at least, to fill his belly. He wouldn't mind shedding his rags or getting out of his mud hut."

"I began to see that," Ilka smiled.

"As the poet Donne said," Singh went on, "no man is an island, and no country is either. The great awakenings you had in Europe, the Renaissance, which liberated man's mind, the rise of democracy, which freed him politically, the industrial revolution, which increased and spread his wealth — news of these things reached Asia. We always had a few intellectuals, you know, who could grasp the significance of this fine ferment in Europe. And though our European rulers, when they took over, tried their best to safeguard us from its influences, their very presence here was bound to quicken our awakening to them. When the British, the French, the Dutch built factories in our cities, even a simpleton gradually became aware of what was up. He knew that they were ruining our cottage industries or handicrafts, the basis of our ancient economy. He learned eventually where the profits went — or at least, where they didn't go. It may not have dawned on the simpleton, but it did on an increasing number of our people, that our foreign masters were here not to help us, but to help themselves. We saw that they were draining what little wealth we had out of us and sending it home.

"That was an economic awakening. The political awakening was bound to follow. Our people had always been poor, as you say. But for the most part, they had always been ruled by their own kind. If the foreigners came and conquered, as once the Mohammedans did, we absorbed them. But it became evident that we could never absorb such strange species of the human race as the British, the French, the Dutch. They were," Singh laughed, "undigestible.

"Remember too that our youth began to go off to Europe to study. The British probably regret it today, but they encouraged it. Probably they thought a European education would help to civilize us, though we had an ancient civilization which, with all its drawbacks, compared favorably, on its spiritual side at least, with Europe's.

"These young men of ours,' Singh went on, "were very happy to find that in England, in France, in Holland a citizen was a free man. And they were thereupon forced to a logical conclusion: if such a state was desirable for a European, was it not equally so for an Asian? Selfishness aside, it was certainly illogical for an Englishman to insist on his own political freedom and deny it to an Indian or a Malayan or a Burmese or a Ceylonese or a Pawancorese. So these young men came home and began to preach their logic. It took fire. It spread. And now, to skip over a thousand details, you see its consequence."

"I do," said Ilka. "I have for some time," she added, a smile breaking on her face. "But I haven't yet told you," she said after a while, "of the change that came over me personally — one similar to yours.

"All those years in Europe and then in Asia I remained the eternal observer. I was increasingly moved by what I saw. It never occurred to me, though, that there might be something, however infinitesimal, I could do about it. Oh, Harold and I — and it meant a certain risk for him in his job — helped quite a few Jews to escape Hitler. We broke a few State Department regulations to give false passports to a handful of intellectuals — Russians, Germans, Spaniards. And beyond such things, to salve my conscience, I took part, as I have told you, in local charity work.

"But it was little. It wasn't enough," Ilka said, and Singh, sensing the climax of her story and excited not only by that but by the realization that this strange and beautiful woman was tearing off a good deal of what remained of the mask that made her such an enigma, gazed at her with rapt attention.

"Singh," she went on, "you live with this evil oppression all of your life, detesting its inhumanity and hoping and praying there will be an end to it. But when there is not, when it goes on and on, and there is no end, no relief in sight, there comes a moment — or at least such a moment came to me, as you say it came to you, when something deep down in you revolts and you are driven in desperation to *do* something, to *participate* in something that will help to destroy this evil, which will replace it with something that in itself is good and desirable and bears hope; and you want to *act* before it is too late, before you die.

"Resolution by itself, I knew," Ilka said, "is still incomplete. It needs an opportunity to transform it into deeds. And that, my dear Singh," she smiled, "is what you have provided. That is what has brought us together — for better or for worse."

"You are not entirely convinced it is for the better?" Singh asked.

"Yes . . ." she replied, half closing her eyes in thought. "I am. I do have my moments of doubt. My position, after all, is quite different from yours. But you have convinced me of one simple truth: that you and your people have the same right to be free as we Americans, or the English. You have the same right to get rid of tyranny as we had, and they had. All my life I've been saying that to people. Now I want to do something about it. If I can help you, Singh, I will do it — anything."

At first she had aided him in his arms-running. Though it sickened her heart to betray Harold Leighton, she had, at the urging of Singh, filched from the consulate-general various official forms of invoices and shipping manifests, consular stamps and seals and stationery, and Singh had made good use of them to camouflage his purchases and to facilitate his correspondence with munition-makers abroad in the face of strict government censorship of the mails. Many a cargo that looked innocent on its ship's manifest was promptly cleared by the sleepy customs authorities at Pawancore

City and then its arms unloaded at night in one of the smaller ports upcountry.

Later, when fighting broke out and Singh had complained that American businessmen in Pawancore were aiding the British, that Chester Groves was beginning to supply them with oil and George Kelly with jeeps and trucks, Ilka had been able to help a group of terrorists whom Singh had recently recruited to take care of that problem. She had got Chester Groves to show her through his oil refinery and had noted which of the great storage tanks were filled. She had carried out a similar reconnaissance in Kelly's vast storehouse, jammed with American motor vehicles, and had been able to tell Singh where a bomb could best be hidden to do the most damage.

Most important of all, Singh thought, Ilka reported to him faithfully every piece of intelligence which came to the American consulate. Thus Singh was able to learn, or confirm, what the governor-general's next moves would be: what reinforcements he expected, how he planned to use them, and recently, what was important above all, that Branhope was contemplating arresting the nationalists leaders, who like Singh were at large in Pawancore City despite the guerilla fighting here and upcountry — arresting them, turning them over to summary courts-martial and stringing a few of them up, as examples. This last information had come to Singh through his own makeshift intelligence service, but he had had his doubts about its accuracy until Ilka got its confirmation through Leighton himself.

Once the news was confirmed, he had made his decision at once and confided it to Ilka, asking her help. At first, she had not believed him; it was merely talk, she thought. Then, when Singh seemed serious, she had refused to have anything to do with it. She would not be an accomplice in cold-blooded murder. That was not the way to win independence. Moreover, it would be senseless for Singh to risk his neck. She would not listen to it. But Singh forced her to, arguing hour after hour on the moral right to kill a despot.

"You would have approved someone getting Stalin or Hitler, wouldn't you?" Singh put it to her.

"Yes, I think I would," Ilka admitted.

"Well, then!" Singh cried.

"I told you Branhope was contemplating this thing, Singh, not that he had definitely decided to do it," Ilka pointed out.

"Very well, then. I am sure that in the end he will come to it — if we hold out as well as we're doing. Therefore we'll make our plans. I think you can help. I mean, I think perhaps you can set it up for us."

"Me!" It was the first time Singh had ever heard her cry out. For Ilka it was the first harrowing glimpse of the precipice, and she shrank from it in terror.

"We will discuss that later," Singh said.

"Promise me this," Ilka said, recovering herself —

"that you will do absolutely nothing until we know definitely that he is going to do this terrible thing."

"It's a promise," Singh said.

The day he learned he was to see the consul-general, apparently about his attentions toward Isobel, of which he felt so ashamed, word had come to Singh that Lord Branhope had made up his mind about the hangings. He drove at once to the Leighton villa — by luck, Isobel was at the country club playing tennis — to see if Ilka could confirm it.

"I will ask Harold when he comes in," she said.

"By the way," Singh said, "does he suspect you?"

"I don't think so," Ilka answered slowly. She had felt herself weighing her answer.

"You're not sure?"

"He has been very uneasy the last few days. He was ill, you know, and his work piled up. And . . ."

"He could talk you out of it — if he knew?" Singh cut in, nervously.

Ilka looked at Singh searchingly, squinting her eyes.

"I don't think so," she said.

Chapter 8

Driving home from Government House late that evening in a torrential downpour, Robert Snow could feel in the damp darkness of the car the utter dejection of his friend. Sporadic flashes of lightning momentarily lit up Leighton's face and Snow caught glimpses of how troubled it was.

What the governor had told them of his plans was depressing enough to both of them, but there must have been something else, Snow was sure, that Lord Branhope had confided to Leighton alone and which had sunk his spirits so low. He suspected what it was, but since Leighton did not mention it he decided to keep his silence. He had done his best the past few days to put the matter out of his friend's mind, and obviously had failed. It was something, Snow realized, that Harold would now have to wrestle with alone — and ultimately with Ilka. He himself had best keep out of it.

It had been a long and ominous evening, Snow thought. At last the governor-general had come to his decisions. Predictable as they were, their very enunciation from the thin lips of this old proconsul, with his finely chiseled aquiline face and his inflexible mind buried in the past century, had at first shocked Snow and then sickened him, as it obviously had Harold Leighton.

The purely military plans were, of course, to be expected. Branhope was receiving reinforcements of two tank battalions, one from India and one from Singapore, and a squadron of light bombers from the Near East. With these he would mop up Pawancore City and the hills back of the capital. After that, when the promised infantry division from home arrived, he would proceed, he had told them, to "pacify" the rest of the country.

In the meantime, Branhope had also confirmed to them, he would declare martial law throughout Pawancore, seize the nationalist leaders, and hale them before courts-martial. Those found guilty of treason would be condemned to the gallows.

"Of course, gentlemen," Lord Branhope had said, "they are all guilty of treason under the law by their very act of leading a rebellion. However, I want to assure my good friend, the American consul-general, who I know is very disturbed at this turn of affairs" — he paused to beam on Leighton — "that I shall exercise clemency in a large number of these cases. But the time has come to make an example of the handful of real culprits, I mean those few who are actually leading the insurrection and especially those who are carrying out sabotage and other acts of terror. I shall show no mercy to them," he added sternly, and it was plain to Leighton and Snow that he meant it.

Both of them had argued strenuously with Branhope against so drastic a measure. He had listened politely and patiently. But his mind was made up, he said.

"I regret the necessity of this as much as you," he told them, "but I have searched my mind and my heart and I see no other way out. I have told these good people time after time that His Majesty's Government is prepared to negotiate an eventual and orderly withdrawal. But they will not listen. They prefer to try to drive us out. One thing they may be sure of. They will fail. They will never get rid of us by force. And as long as we are here we shall enforce, to the utmost of our power, law and order."

Snow had gazed on the elderly gentleman with a certain fascination, revolted as he was at the thought of the dreadful consequences of such arbitrariness. He marveled at Branhope's poise, the dry tone of his voice, the lack of any sign of emotion in his finely bred, aristocratic face, the absence of any doubt whatsoever that he was doing what was right, what any Christian gentleman would feel duty bound to do in the circumstances. Branhope, Snow knew by instinct, would be the kindliest of men toward his dogs and his horses. He was undoubtedly considerate to his servants and to the swarm of officials who served him in the government. He had an old-fashioned gallantry towards women. And Snow knew that he not only gave liberally to dozens of charities in Pawancore but took an unusually active part in furthering their work. There were several "Lord Branhope Funds" for the poor which were especially dear to the old man's heart. And yet — Snow tried to comprehend it — this man could send others to the gallows, men who were considered patriots throughout the length and breadth of this steaming land, without a quiver of his fine eyebrows.

It had fascinated Snow too — and gladdened his heart — to observe the compassion which Harold Leighton had shown in his arguments with the governor. Harold was eloquent in expressing his understanding and sympathy for Branhope's difficult position. But he pled with him not to resort to cold-blooded murder. The slaughter among the poorly armed Sikhs and Hindus when the tanks and bombers went into action would be frightful enough, but that was the price of war. But to court-martial the leading men of this country, who surely later would be hailed as heroes, patriots and martyrs who wanted only what he and Lord Branhope wanted for their own people and who, like themselves, were ready to fight for it — to court-martial them and string them up on the gallows seemed to him to be nothing less than calculated murder. It would not only arouse Asia, but decent people throughout the West.

"You say, sir," Leighton said, "that the example will

dampen the spirit of rebellion in these people, and bring them around to reason — that is, to your point of view. In my opinion it will have the opposite effect. It will deepen their resentment. It will arouse them to increased defiance. It will breed more outright terror. They will strike back, sir, all the harder."

And Leighton had ended, Snow was pleased to see, on a constructive note, urging the governor to take the initiative in resuming negotiations.

"An impartial observer cannot help but conclude," he argued, "that there is only one major point of difference between you and these nationalists."

"And what is that, my dear Leighton?" Branhope said, genially enough.

"The time limit for your departure," Leighton said quickly. "Set any reasonable date you wish, Governor. But set a date. I am convinced it will be accepted."

"That, my dear fellow," Branhope said, "is a matter for London to decide."

"But you, sir," Leighton rejoined, "with your immense influence, could induce London to accept almost any date you think reasonable."

"I'm afraid that is beyond my province, Leighton." And with that the governor had dismissed the subject.

"It was his one outright evasion of the evening," Snow said to Leighton as their car approached the Leighton villa.

"I felt so too," Leighton said, breaking his long silence.

"It's disastrous, what he proposes to do," Snow said.

"Yes."

"The hangings, I mean."

"Yes," Leighton echoed. It was obvious to Snow that disturbed as his friend was about them, his thoughts were now on something else — on the other thing, no doubt. Snow recalled that for the last half-hour before they departed Branhope and Leighton had retired to the governor's study, and that when Harold had emerged, his face was laden with anguish.

As the car entered the driveway, Snow felt Harold taking his arm.

"Bob, if Ilka is still up, I would like to speak to her alone — if you don't mind."

They found Ilka Leighton sitting up in the living room, and Snow noticed immediately that the ash tray at her side was piled with cigarette butts. Next to it was a half-empty bottle of Scotch — it must have been the one he had opened himself for a quick highball before going out to dinner. However, she showed no sign of having imbibed so much. She put her book down and greeted them quietly. Snow started to excuse himself.

"Won't you have a nightcap with us first, Bob?" she asked.

"Not tonight, my dear," Snow said. "I had more than my full quota at the governor's."

"I hope Harold was careful," Ilka smiled, turning to

her husband. "You're still a convalescent, you know, darling."

"I was quite abstemious, my dear," Leighton said, and Snow watched his attempt to smile. Harold, it was obvious, was striving fiercely to keep himself under control. Ilka, Bob thought, must have noticed it but she gave no inkling of being apprehensive. In her white silk sleeveless dress, which bared the fine molding of her shoulders and arms, she seemed cool and composed despite the unbearable mugginess of the night, but of course, Snow reflected, no one ever knew what might be boiling inside this imperturbable being. The heap of cigarette ends, it occurred to him, and the half-drained bottle of Scotch were visible evidence that something might well be boiling, or at least smoldering. He bent down and kissed her, said "Good night," and, depressed at having to leave them in such an ominous state, left the room.

Leighton sat down on the divan beside his wife.

"You look exhausted, dear," she said. "Perhaps a small one won't hurt you." She got up to pour him a drink.

"How did you make out with Isobel?" Leighton said.

"I tried to reassure her, poor thing," Ilka said, handing Leighton the drink and sitting down. "But she is beyond helping — for the moment."

"She'll get over it."

"Of course."

"Did you talk to Singh?" Leighton said, looking for the first time squarely at Ilka.

"Isobel insisted that I talk to him." She met his eyes without a second's hesitation. "I told him frankly I thought it was a little shabby the way he had misled her."

"Was he angry with you?"

Ilka smiled. "No," she said.

Leighton lit a cigarette and puffed it silently for a moment. "He's on the governor's list."

"Singh? What list?" She did not raise her voice as Leighton, eyeing her carefully now, had expected.

"We had quite an evening," Leighton said.

"Do tell me about it. I'm quite curious, you know," Ilka said, reaching for a cigarette which Leighton bent over to light for her.

"The old man has finally made up his mind — as I mentioned to you earlier this evening."

"To what?" Ilka asked, and Leighton thought there was more contempt than apprehension in her voice.

"He's going to drive the nationalists out of the city, to begin with."

"With what?"

"He's getting in a couple of battalions of tanks and some light bombers."

"From where?"

"From India and Malaya. The bombers, I think he said, are coming out from the Near East."

"I see," Ilka said, taking a long draw on her cigarette and inhaling the smoke. "That looks bad, doesn't it?"

"Very bad," Leighton said. "With tanks and bombers, Branhope will slaughter them." Leighton turned intently to his wife. "But he is going to do something else much worse!"

"What?"

"I think I mentioned it to you just before I left," Leighton said. He was thinking that he must soon get to the point. Perhaps there would be a natural opening now.

"The governor is going to declare martial law. He says he intends to arrest all the nationalist leaders he can get his hands on, and turn them over to courts-martial. The verdicts, he admits, will be automatic. He . . ."

"Automatic?" Ilka interrupted.

"Well, under the law, you're guilty of treason if you lead an armed rebellion."

"He is going to hang all these people, then?" Ilka asked, and now, he saw, her calm was gone; her black eyes were dilating.

"No. He said he would exercise his right of clemency in most of the cases. But he would show no mercy toward those actually leading the guerillas or carrying out sabotage or any other isolated acts of terror."

"You mentioned a list. You said Singh . . ."

"Branhope showed me the first list to be arrested. It includes all members of the Supreme Council. Singh, of

[114]

course, is on it — as a member of the Council. But I gather the old man suspects, as I've told you before, that Singh is mixed up with the terrorists, perhaps is their secret leader. If he's right, Singh is in for some real trouble."

"They might hang him?" Ilka asked, and Leighton felt her struggling to keep her voice low.

"Yes," Leighton said. "They might."

Ilka crushed the end of her cigarette, lit a new one before Leighton could get out his lighter and gulped at her highball, emptying the half-filled glass. She sat back, blowing smoke in billows halfway across the room and staring at the opposite wall. Then, to Harold's surprise, she seemed abruptly to change her mood. She sat back on the divan and took his hand.

"After all, Harold," she said in a low, almost relaxed tone, "I suppose it is none of our business what happens here."

Leighton saw the opening and took his plunge.

"Ilka!" he fairly cried, pressing her hand.

"Yes?" she said calmly, when he hesitated.

"Would you say that you were not making it your business!"

"What do you mean, Harold?"

"I mean . . . Ilka, I am obliged to ask you . . . the most painful question that has ever risen in our lifetime . . . My dear, are you in any way involved in this thing?"

He was ashamed at the trembling of his voice, but at least he had got the words out that had been too long unspoken. He gazed at her so imploringly that it was as if, Ilka felt, his life depended on her answer. Perhaps, in a way, it did, and her's too, the thought flashed over her quickly and was as quickly rejected. It was too soon to say that.

"What thing?" she responded, with as innocent an expression on her face as Leighton had ever seen.

"This trouble here . . . This nationalist uprising . . . All the things this young Singh is up to . . ." He groped for words.

"Harold, you amaze me. How on earth could I, the wife of the American consul-general, be involved in that?"

"That's what I told him."

"Who?"

"I told him it was absurd . . . The governor."

"So it was His Excellency," Ilka smiled, contempt rising in her voice and face.

"He mentioned it to me on more than one occasion, Ilka."

"And obviously this evening."

"Yes."

"And what, may I ask, am I specifically accused of?"

Leighton did not answer at once. He got up and strode to the window, peered out toward the blackness of the rain-swept night, turned back toward Ilka, studied for a second her inscrutable face to see if there were not some hint of a clue, and standing before her said:

"Ilka, how well do you know Govind Singh?"

"How well?"

"Yes."

"It is difficult to say," Ilka answered, in a matter-of-fact tone. "I have seen much less of him than you have."

"But somehow . . ."

"Somehow I feel I know him rather well," Ilka said. "You remember, we discussed that earlier this evening."

"Yes, when I said that in regard to Isobel you saw through him all the time, that you obviously knew him better than I. You made me wonder, Ilka."

"You recall what I said?" Ilka asked.

"Yes. You said it was a woman's instinct. Is that all?"

"Not all. No," Ilka said. "Like you, I admire Singh. His intelligence. His courage. His standing for something, and doing something about it. We've never known too many people like that, Harold."

"That is true." Leighton sat down again beside her. He was not getting very far. Perhaps he conceded, he never would, with her.

"Tell me, Ilka." He would make one more attempt. "These matters I discuss with you . . . the information that comes into the office . . . you keep them quite to yourself, don't you?"

"Quite."

"Singh is a persuasive fellow."

"I've seen him worm a great deal out of you, Harold," Ilka smiled.

"Nothing confidential, I hope," Leighton said, matching her smile. He glanced at his watch. "I'm afraid, my dear, I am keeping you up fearfully late."

"I'm not sleepy. Are you?"

"No. Just tired."

"Perhaps we should turn in," she said, but neither made a move to get up.

"Shall we have just one more — a small one?" Harold asked, rising to his feet. As he picked out the ice cubes and mixed the drinks, he felt her gazing at him quizzically.

"Harold," she said. "You put thoughts in my head."

"Yes?" Looking at her profile, the classic lines from her fine forehead down the eyes, the straight nose, the full lips, the adequate chin, to the curve of the throat, he felt a quiver of excitement pass through him. He had gazed on it a thousand times, perhaps ten thousand times, but it was always new, fresh, provocative.

"Supposing I were up to something? Would it be wrong to help these people here?" she said, half closing her eyes.

"That would depend," Harold said.

"On what?"

"On what you did."

"You could be wrong, you mean, in doing right?"

"Yes, you could," Harold said. "On the other hand, I think you will admit, Ilka, that what I have done for these people — the pressure I've brought, and got our government to bring, on the British to settle this thing as soon as possible, little as it may have been, was both right and proper."

"You have done a great deal," Ilka said. "No one else I know in our foreign service would have done half as much. But, Harold, haven't you failed?"

"Not entirely." Leighton smiled good-naturedly. "I think I can say, Ilka, that I've speeded up the timetable. I told Branhope just this evening that if he would only set a definite date — any reasonable date, just so it was specific — I was sure the leaders here would accept it and end this useless war. I honestly believe the governor is beginning to see that."

"Has any people ever been *given* its freedom — and on a timetable?" Ilka asked. "In your own American revolution, weren't there a lot of British promises about granting freedom?"

"That was a long time ago. And anyway the situation in Asia is quite different."

"Is it?" Ilka said. "Isn't it the same old thing? People want to rule themselves, here as elsewhere. And to do so, don't they, in the end, have to resort to force, as your people did?"

Suddenly Leighton thought he saw the light.

"Ilka! Are you trying to justify yourself!"

[119]

"I'm trying to understand something," Ilka said, not raising her voice.

Leighton felt completely frustrated. "All I hope, my dear," he blurted out, "is that you are not going to do something foolish."

"I have no thought of doing anything foolish, I promise you that," Ilka said softly.

"To put it on a purely selfish basis," Harold said, "it could wreck my career."

Ilka regarded him intently, and he wondered what thoughts were rushing through her strange mind.

"It's your life, isn't it?"

"What's my life?" he said, not trying to hide his impatience.

"Your work. Your career."

"That — and you. Yes, that is my life. My work. You. Isobel."

"What you believe in — isn't that your life too?" Ilka asked. Leighton was puzzled at her self-possession.

"Yes," he said. "I suppose it is. Naturally."

"Perhaps that is the most important thing," Ilka said softly, "in any of our lives."

Leighton stared at her, conscious of trying to repress a feeling of terror that was mounting through his veins.

"Ilka!" he cried. "For the first time in our marriage, you frighten me!"

Chapter 9

SINGH WENT into hiding.

Before the posters were up on the walls of the town the next evening announcing the arrest and the impending court-martial of some fifty nationalist leaders, he had slipped quietly away from his home and his office and, thoroughly disguised, had found refuge in a place that Ilka was certain would be safe for the time being. She felt confident that she alone knew of his whereabouts and she was relieved that it enabled them to see one another daily. It gave her control, she assured herself, over what might happen, for she knew, despite Singh's protestations of iron determination, that she had not finally made up her mind by any means.

Each day brought fresh doubts in her mind, but she tried to down them by throwing herself into the work of preparing for the farewell garden party on the Fourth of July, which was but a few days off, and in beginning to pack for their departure. There were letters to write to friends back in Washington, apprising them of the Leightons' coming and begging them to keep their eyes open for a small house in Georgetown. And there was Isobel to console.

In fact, and she was thankful for it, there were a great many things to help ease the strain. There was a dinner for the two frenetic businessmen, Chester Groves and George Kelly, who were making Harold's life miserable with their unreasonable demands. And the Leightons were to dine at Government House on July second. It would be an intimate affair, Harold had said, with only themselves present — the governor wanted to have a friendly, personal farewell get-together with them alone. That would be an ordeal, coming only two days before the Fourth, and she would have to be very careful.

But nowhere more than in her own household. For as the days ticked by a sickening fear grew in her that Harold or Bob Snow or Isobel — or all three of them — might recognize Singh despite a disguise that made him quite unrecognizable to her except when he approached her and dropped the rather falsetto voice he had assumed and the obsequious manners of an Oriental household servant doubling at odd jobs in the kitchen and in the garden.

It had been Singh's idea and it had seemed to her at first to be so ingenious that scarcely any risk at all was involved, and ingenious too because it provided not only sanctuary for this hunted man but eventually, in a few days, the opportunity which they sought, or which he sought. Certainly the residence of the American consul-general would be the last place in Pawancore that the authorities would think of searching for Singh.

She had substituted him for one of the Sikh servants who had been asking for a month's leave so that he could visit his family in his native village a hundred miles north in the hills. The man's wife had had another baby that he was curious, he said, to see. So Janji Singh had been replaced temporarily by Govind Singh. Almost all Sikh men, it seemed to Ilka, were called Singh, and Govind Singh had explained once, she seemed to recall, that it was actually not a name but a title, and meant "lion." Singh — her Singh, who fancied himself as something of an amateur actor — quickly made himself accepted among the numerous domestics, concocting a broad north-country accent and comporting himself like a peasant.

He was indeed something to look at! The very sight of him at first reduced Ilka to tears of laughter. He had a long black false beard which hid his face except for the eyes and the nose, and which he managed to tie to his wig of long black hair under a rolled turban; and he wore long shorts in the orthodox Sikh manner. She could never make him out among the servants until he came close to her and reverted to his natural voice.

This occurred daily in the garden, which Singh was busy tidying up for the Fourth of July. The lawn had to be mowed, the flower beds weeded, the bushes trimmed, and Singh threw himself into the work with typical abandon. There was time, though, when Ilka went out to "supervise" his tasks, for talk. By the end of June, Singh had formulated his plans and Ilka had listened to them without specifically committing herself, though she was aware that Singh assumed that she had. If he could act completely alone, she would probably not stand in his way. But he was counting on her to play a crucial part, and the more he talked of it, the more she shrank away. Only, she could not summon the courage to tell him. It would be cowardly, it would be a betrayal, to go back on him now. Yet, if she were not a coward, she was not its opposite, whatever you called it, either. Despite what others — Singh, first of all, and Harold and Snow and others — thought, she was really lacking in true valor. She had all the weaknesses of a woman — why didn't the others see that?

"It will be a very simple thing," Singh said one afternoon when the rains had let up and he was puttering in the garden. "I have worked it all out in my mind. The people will be milling around out here. Right?"

"If it is not raining," Ilka said.

"We will discuss that later. To begin with, you can arrange for me to be one of the waiters."

"You would drop your tray!" Ilka tried to laugh.

"You must overlook my deficiencies, madame," Singh smiled. "I have figured it out this way." He began to talk rapidly and tensely. "I will carry about the glasses of champagne. Toward the end, you will get him aside. Propose a toast. You will beckon me for the champagne. I shall come up. You step aside. And in that instant, it is done!"

"It sounds almost too easy," Ilka said, evasively.

"It will not be difficult," Singh said.

"Aren't there a lot of things that could happen that would spoil such a plan?"

"Yes. But I shall try to take them into consideration. We still have a few days to think of them. Can you think of any yourself?"

"No," Ilka said. "But there are bound to be some. Nothing ever comes off just as you plan it, Singh."

"This will — I am sure of it. There are two things to watch out for. You must draw the old man completely aside — perhaps find some pretext to lead him back to the veranda, or better still, to the living room. That is most important. We don't want any innocent ones in the way. Second, and even more important. You, your-self, madame, must step well away, at the last moment. You understand?"

"Yes," she said vaguely. She was trying to summon the strength to tell him that the whole thing was out of the question, that she was too frail in spirit, that she could never go through with it, and that they must not take the fatal risk of exposing him at the moment when she would surely flinch. But a sudden flash of his humor threw her off.

"I emphasize that," he smiled, "because I am not a very good shot. I am not William Tell."

On the last day of June, the reinforcements began to arrive from India and Singapore, and some of the tank units went into action almost immediately in the dock area where the nationalists were dug in. At first the tanks were used mostly as artillery to blast away at the old buildings. But their crews, Bob Snow noticed as he watched the action from Leighton's second-story office in the consulate, must not have been in combat recently, for their aim was wild and by early afternoon stray shells from their 75-millimeter cannon had set fire to Chester Groves's oil refinery along the bay south of the docks and scored three direct hits on the great warehouse, north of the docks, where George Kelly stored his motor vehicles, sending it too up in flames.

At dinner that evening at the Leighton villa, both businessmen fairly erupted. Where was the protection of the flag! The Stars and Stripes, which had proudly waved over American property, had been shot down! It was aggression against the U.S.A.! What was the American consul-general doing about it! Had he notified Washington of this wanton act! Had he called for help — for destroyers, a cruiser, bombers! To help put down this rebellion! And compel respect for American business interests! The United States must intervene — and at once!

Disturbed as he was about what had happened — the loss would probably run into a million dollars — and sympathetic as he was to the plight of the two aroused men, Leighton knew that there was precious little that an American consul-general could do. Both businessmen knew it too, or would if they could calm down a little. If you got caught in the middle of a battle, you were liable to get hurt, no matter how innocent you were. And Groves and Kelly were naturally in a state of confusion. They were heaping the blame on the "rebels" and demanding that the U.S.A. help put them down; yet the damage had been done by British shells.

"We can file claims for compensation from the government," Leighton said, seeking to bring some encouragement to the two men. "You can prove, can't you, that it was the shells from the tanks that did the damage?"

The idea seemed to cheer up both Groves and Kelly a little, or at least to reduce their hysteria.

"What else could it have been?" Groves said. "The natives don't have any artillery, do they?"

"It was those seventy-five-millimeter cannon on the tanks that got me," Kelly said.

He was a hot-tempered, ruddy-complexioned, red-headed Irishman from Brooklyn, with as open a face as Leighton had ever seen. He could blow up, Harold had found, on the slightest pretext, but he was essentially a decent, generous man who subsided as quickly as he flared up. He was quite oblivious to politics, or at least to what was going on in Asia. He had come out here to sell cars, jeeps, trucks, bulldozers and tractors, and the only thing he understood about the uprising in Pawancore was that it had threatened to destroy his business until the government authorities, in recent weeks, had begun giving him sizable orders. As a matter of fact, Leighton had noted, Kelly liked the Pawancore people — he liked people he did business with — and had trained a notable band of Sikhs and Hindus to service his vehicles and to operate the bulldozers, the tractors, the trucks without destroying them. He had been proud of the skill and the loyalty of these men, and had been both puzzled and hurt when most of them drifted away over the past few months to join the nationalist forces. Kelly had had two reasons, Leighton knew, for not particularly liking the English out here. First, he was an Irishman; second, he had had to contend with a good deal of discrimination against him by the government, which naturally favored British firms which handled British vehicles. To overcome this, Leighton had been of great help, as had Govind Singh, who had been Kelly's lawyer. Kelly regarded both as his friends. He would, as he said, do anything for them — and for Mrs. Leighton, whom he revered.

Chester Groves had been more difficult for Leighton to deal with. He seemed to have all the unpleasant characteristics of the Texas oil men one read about in the novels. A big, driving man with a hawkish expression about his sunburned face, he was loud-mouthed, thick-skinned, aggressive and intolerant, and apparently lived under the misapprehension that the oil business was the center of the universe. That he was able, and behind the rhinoceros hide of his exterior, shrewd and intelligent in his operations, Leighton freely conceded. It would have been child's play to butter up the native officials of Pawancore but Groves, some years back, had been able to convince the governor-general himself that he was the man to exploit Pawancore's suspected oil resources. Now that he had succeeded in exploiting them, nothing else mattered to him, and the "rebellion" as he called it, appeared in his eyes as an impertinence that had to be crushed because it was seriously interfering with what he was doing, and threatening his very considerable investment. He had had some experience of this kind once in Mexico and, as he said, it had cost him a "few millions" to learn what happened when the "Bolsheviks" were not put quickly down. To Groves all the trouble in the world, all the threats against constituted authority, were made by "communists," and once when Leighton had tried to explain to him that fortunately in Pawancore, as in India, the revolution was "nationalist" and not "communist," the oil man had looked at the consul-general as though he suspected that Leighton were a secret emissary of Stalin. His shrewdness and intelligence, Harold concluded, obviously did not ex-

[129]

tend to politics; they were confined to extracting oil out of the earth, at a profit.

That Groves had a poor opinion of the consul-general, he scarcely concealed from Leighton. And Bob Snow relayed enough of the oil man's bilious sentiments to his friend to provide adequate confirmation.

"I hope you will tell the bastard to go jump into the bay," Snow said. He and Leighton and Ilka were snatching a quiet drink before the businessmen arrived for dinner. "In fact, that's what I told him myself this afternoon after listening patiently for an hour to his goddamned — excuse me, Ilka — unmitigated tripe. Of course, he was in a frenzy about what had happened to the refinery. You could sympathize with him for that. But he blamed you for it, Harold!"

"Me?" Leighton smiled.

"You know his line. He has inflicted it on me ever since I came out. He says you're not protecting American interests out here. He says you're a goddamned long-hair, that you have no business being a consul. That what we need — 'we' being he — is a businessman type, aggressive, a fighter, who will stand for no nonsense from the natives.

" 'Who set your plant on fire anyway?' I said. 'The natives?'

" 'No. But they're the cause of all the trouble,' he screamed. 'And what have we got for a consul-general out here?' he went on. 'A guy who is sympathetic to these rebels! He told me so himself. And his wife is worse. If you ask me, she's more than sympathetic. A fine couple to be representing America out here!'"

Snow saw Leighton's face drop, and he regretted having let the last remark slip out. He glanced quickly at Ilka; she was smiling.

"How do I come in?" she asked.

"He resents you — didn't you know it? . . ."

"I knew," she said, her smile broadening.

". . . Because you're a 'foreigner,' he says. A week or so ago," Snow went on, "I let him rave for an hour on that subject.

"'That's another thing against Leighton,' he said. 'He's married to a foreigner!'

"'She's the most wonderful woman I ever knew' — I defended you, Ilka dear," Snow laughed. "'And besides,' I said, 'she has been an American citizen for twenty-five years, and a damned good one.'

"'She comes from one of those cheap countries in Eastern Europe, doesn't she?' Groves said.

"'From Hungary,' I said. 'A fine little country, full of beautiful women. Besides, Groves,' I said, 'There's oil there, I think. You ought to visit it some time.'

"But the so-and-so persisted. 'I thought American diplomats,' he said, 'were forbidden by law to marry foreigners.'

"'They weren't when the Leightons were married — thank God!' I said.

" 'Well, they ought to have been.' "

Despite their state of excitement, the two guests displayed a healthy appetite, Ilka noted, gobbling down their food between a running fire of talk.

"Any word from Washington?" Groves asked, gripping his fork as if he were ready to plunge it into Leighton.

"I cabled a full account of what happened," Leighton said. "But there has hardly been time for a reply."

"Did you contact the Navy, Harold?" Kelly asked.

"A consul has to act through the State Department, George," Leighton said.

"So we don't get any Naval help — not even a destroyer," Groves said, his eyes full of hostility.

"Do you really expect that, Chester?" Leighton turned to him.

"I expect our government to at least try to protect American business interests," Groves snapped.

"A destroyer would help," Kelly said.

He was already calming down, Leighton noticed. The idea of American intervention here was so absurd that it scarcely needed explaining to two adult men. Perhaps in Latin America in the old days, where Groves had made his first killings in oil, a Navy gunboat or a company of Marines had intervened with the desired effect. In Asia, or at least in large parts of it such as China, a frigate or two once had been all that was necessary to cow the natives and force them to trade on Western terms. But those days were over. Today, with Asia in such ferment, a Yankee businessman accepted certain risks. He could not expect the government in Washington to bail him out whenever revolution broke out. Groves and Kelly ought to know that. But he would repeat, Leighton decided, what he had been telling them the last few weeks.

"Gentlemen, I think you realize as well as I," he said, speaking softly, "that our government does not intend to interfere in any of these places out here where the European authorities are having their troubles."

"We're helping the nationalists in China, aren't we?" Groves cut in.

"Yes. But China is not ruled by any foreign power. Or would you want us," Leighton added with a twinkle in his eyes, "to help the nationalists here?"

Groves's answer was a cold stare, but Kelly smiled.

"Much as an Irishman hates 'em," Kelly said, "I think we ought to help the British out of this mess. They certainly need help."

"They wouldn't accept it. You know that, George."

"Too proud, eh?"

"That is part of it, perhaps," Leighton said.

"Well, if you won't do anything for us," Grove said belligerently, "I think I know some senators back home who will."

Leighton smiled. "I don't see how they can, Chester."

"You'll see. And by the way, Harold," Groves added,

"the Senate has to approve your new appointment, doesn't it?"

"No. I don't think so, Chester. Why?"

"I just wondered," Groves said, and the others caught the malevolent look in his eyes.

Bob Snow spoke up. "I take it that both you gentlemen are fully covered by insurance."

"That's what I have to find out," Kelly said.

"No insurance can compensate me for the production I'm going to lose," Chester Groves said.

"That reminds me," Kelly said. "Has anyone seen our Singh? I tried to get him all afternoon."

"I believe he has gone into hiding," Snow said. "To escape arrest and possible court-martial."

"I hope the governor strings him up — with the rest of them," Groves snorted.

"Not Singh, man! He's my lawyer. He's got to go to work on these claims for me," Kelly retorted.

"I'm afraid you're out of luck there, George," Leighton said. "But perhaps we can help you out at the consulate."

"What happened to the man?"

"I don't know," Leighton answered. "As far as I know he left no traces."

"The governor is really going to be tough this time, isn't he?" Groves turned to Leighton.

"I'm afraid he is."

"Afraid? It was high time, wasn't it?"

Ilka watched her husband intently. He had handled the despicable Groves so well, she thought. He had not flinched from revealing what he thought. All along, his sympathies had been with the people here. How had she strayed from him? Out of what impatience? What folly? And now he was going to tell this worm of a businessman, who was interested only in his profits, who cared nothing for people as human beings, what he thought of the governor's hangings. What a decent, courageous, admirable, lovable man Harold was!

"I advised him against it," Harold said.

"The hell you did!" Groves exploded.

"In fact, I pled with him — until I was blue in the face." Leighton raised his voice and Ilka saw the color rising in his tired face and making it come wonderfully to life. "It is not only a mistake," I told him, "to court-martial these people and hang some of them. It is cold-blooded murder."

"They did it in Ireland." Kelly spoke up to everyone's surprise. "It's in their blood, I'm tellin' you."

"I thought you said we had no business intervening in this thing," Groves said sarcastically.

"There are some things a friendly foreign government and its representative can legitimately do," Leighton answered. "It is no secret that the United States for some years now has brought pressure on London to honor its promises here, as well as in India."

"But it is not our affair. You've said so a hundred times. You're always saying it," Groves persisted.

"It is not wrong to influence others," Harold said.

"And pressure them? I believe you used that term."

"That too. I, of course, Chester, do not make policy. In a small way, my job is to carry it out. But I must say I've been in complete sympathy with it."

"On what grounds, may I ask, sir?" Groves said.

"We Americans have always been against colonialism. We have always believed a people — any people — should govern themselves. I suppose that is why we brought pressure — and admittedly and understandably it was not always welcome — on our British friends to get out of Pawancore, and out of India. I've been glad to do my part here.

"Some people," Leighton went on, glancing good-naturedly at his wife, "think I have failed. Perhaps I have. It would appear so. But actually there is only one point of difference between the governor and these nationalists — a definite timetable for withdrawal. If we can get our friends to agree to that, there will be a settlement."

"I cannot see old Branhope surrendering to this riff-raff," Groves said. "And I say thank God for that!"

"An agreement to do the inevitable is not a surrender," Leighton smiled.

"So you think these rebels will win!" Groves exclaimed.

"In the long run I think these people will get what they want — yes."

"Not if the old man hangs enough of them!"

"I'm still hoping he will have enough sense — and humanity — not to," Harold said, and Ilka, pride swelling within her, saw how Leighton was struggling to keep his emotions in check. "Enough sense, I say, because such brutal repression will boomerang on him. It will make these people more determined than ever to push him out. It will drive them to stop at nothing to achieve that.

"And humanity enough, I say, because no struggle, no war, no revolution, however obscene, and whatever the stakes, justifies calculated murder of individuals by either side."

Ilka Leighton found it difficult that night to ease herself into sleep. It was not the heat or the humidity, though both were oppressive. She could not get Harold's closing remarks at dinner out of her head.

. . . *We have always believed a people — any people — should govern themselves . . . I was glad to do my part . . . In the long run these people will get what they want . . . I'm still hoping there will be no hangings . . . Nothing, however obscene, whatever the stakes, justifies cold-blooded murder of individuals by either side. . . .*

He was so eloquent, so moving, so right. Tomorrow,

as soon as the others had cleared out, she must go to Singh in the garden. She must tell him that it was impossible; that she would not go through with it; that he could not do it; that it was wrong. She must tell him that he would have to go. He must not be here on the Fourth of July!

Chapter 10

Bᴜᴛ Sɪɴɢʜ was beyond listening.

Ilka found him half concealed in a hedge kneeling over the morning paper. "Just as I told you," he said, pointing to the headlines with his pruning shears.

"What?" she said. She had not yet seen the morning paper.

"The first court-martial. It begins this morning."

"Singh, I've been thinking . . ." Ilka started to say.

"So have I, madame. I've worked it all out."

"I mean —"

"The important thing," he interrupted, "is to get the old man away from the others. You must think of some pretext. You must entice him onto the veranda, and then lead him into the living room. That is where we will do it. No one will see. You will be perfectly safe. No one will suspect you."

"And you?"

"Don't worry about me," Singh smiled.

"I do. Every minute. What will you do?"

"I shall dash into the kitchen. There will be a car waiting outside. The consul-general's, in fact!"

"Singh!"

"It will be easy to get away."

"Singh, I can't!"

"You will, though. I am confident."

"I'm weakening."

"It is too late for that," Singh said.

"You should have listened to my husband last night."

"Did you promise him anything?"

"No."

"Does he know?"

"No."

"Suspect?"

"I don't think so," Ilka said. "Not this, anyway. He is troubled about me, in a general way."

"You can have a clean conscience," Singh said.

"My God, how!"

"What will you be guilty of? You merely invite the gentleman into the house. There is no crime in that, madame."

"You know there is," Ilka said.

"No court could prove it."

"That I was an accomplice?"

Singh stood up, his dark eyes suddenly flashing. "There is one thing I want you to understand! You are never to admit anything! I shall never open my mouth — even if they get me and give me the works."

"Why should I get out of it?"

"I insist! Otherwise it is off!"

Ilka tried to smile. "So far as I'm concerned, Singh, it *is* off. But not because of that. Last night Harold talked very movingly. He is on your side. He said he knew you would get what you want. Soon. And he convinced me that cold-blooded murder of any individual by either side is wrong."

"Even if the other side does it first?"

"The governor, as I keep reminding you, Singh, has not hanged anyone yet."

"Look at the headlines here," Singh said impatiently, pounding at them with his shears. "The first courts-martial. Tomorrow you will read of the first hangings."

"I doubt it. Even if there are death sentences, Stanhope will commute them."

"He won't, though," Singh said. "You know that."

"He must! Singh," Ilka said. "Harold and I are dining with him tomorrow — alone. We shall find out."

"Good. That makes it easy, then. We shall know definitely — before the Fourth."

Ilka started to turn to go. "One more thing," Singh said. "Could you make sure, when you see him tomorrow, that he is coming here?"

"I shall remind him of it," Ilka said.

A feeling of helplessness overwhelmed her as she walked slowly back to the villa. She had said it was off, but he had not understood, and she had not tried very hard to make him understand. Why? Why had her resolve melted? Why had she not had the courage to make it clear to him? As she mounted the steps to the veranda she remembered that she was going to suggest that he leave. She had even rehearsed the argument in her mind: that it was not fair to Harold Leighton for him to remain here, that if he were discovered it could destroy her husband's career. An appeal to Singh's sense of honor, which was of the highest, would be sure to succeed. And if Singh left, all her problems, her terrible dilemma, the haunting temptation, would be resolved. There was still time — four days until the Fourth.

That afternoon the first bombers came over, barely clearing the trees that fringed the garden where the Leightons and a few guests were having tea. They could hear, a moment later, the explosions from the dock area.

"It's murder!" Bob Snow exclaimed.

"If the nationalists had a little flak, they would knock them off like sitting ducks," Everett Willoughby, the young vice-consul, said. It was not, Leighton mused, that Willoughby meant to express any sympathy for the nationalists — he was too careful for that. He was simply talking as an expert; he had served in the Air Force the last year or two of the recent war.

"I suppose you met plenty of flak in Germany." Leighton turned to him.

"The Germans made it pretty hot for us, sir. They made us fly pretty high."

Willoughby — and Leighton was grateful to him — had been very helpful the past few days with Isobel. He had taken her out nearly every afternoon to play tennis at the country club and had squired her to various parties in the evenings. He was certainly taking her mind — if not her heart — off preoccupation with Singh. In fact she had mentioned Singh only once to him in the past few days; she had asked if her father had any idea where she might write to him.

"It's a strange kind of warfare, isn't it?" Willoughby said.

"It's certainly unequal," Snow said. "What kind of a chance have these people against bombers?"

"I mean, it seems strange," Willoughby said, "to be able to have a sort of grandstand seat to watch it. In Berlin, I doubt if anyone, outside of the antiaircraft gunners and the roof spotters, ever saw us. It would have been too dangerous. The inhabitants, quite sensibly, took to the shelters. But here we sit and sip tea and look on, like at a show."

"It's the same way with the fighting down in the port," Snow said. "I watch it nearly every day from a grandstand seat in Harold's office. It's as safe, and the view of the action is as good, as if you were sitting in Yankee Stadium."

"Not since those bloody tanks got into the show,"

Kelly said. "They don't know where they're shooting."

"Maybe they do," Snow laughed. "Maybe they knew you were an Irishman."

"They sure fixed me," Kelly smiled.

The planes, a dozen of them, zoomed overhead coming back from the dock area, and already from the lawn one could see a vast cloud of smoke rising from the city below.

"Mr. Leighton, sir! You've got to get me out of here!" A stentorian voice spoke out.

For forty-eight hours now, Leighton had had a new problem on his hands. A United States Senator had flown in, unannounced, on the courier plane from Delhi and was now stranded. The commercial lines had abruptly ceased service in and out of Pawancore City until the trouble should subside. Apparently some trigger-happy guerillas had taken a few shots at a passenger plane coming in for a landing the week before. And because of the fighting in the port area, the sailings of the British and French passenger boats had been canceled until further notice. Leighton had wired Delhi to send the courier plane back to fetch the anxious senator, but he had not received a reply.

"We shall find a way to get you out, Senator," Leighton tried to assure him. He had had long experience with junketing Congressmen. One had to be especially attentive to senators. They were not — most of them — very friendly to the foreign service, but they had to approve your appointment if you ever were named a minister.

"No reply from Delhi yet?" Senator Bridgehorn asked.

"Not yet, Senator. But I expect one in the morning. Either that, or the plane itself."

"Don't you find it interesting here, sir?" Bob Snow inquired. Senators — some senators, at any rate — were dear to him because they provided such excellent targets for his somewhat acid pen.

"I had no idea what I was getting into, sir," Senator Bridgehorn muttered. "Our consul-general in Delhi did not tell me. He will be sorry for that, I think."

"I did not know myself," Leighton said, "that the bombing would start today."

"I have no confidence in the British Air Force — in its accuracy, I mean," Senator Bridgehorn said. He had a booming voice and he used it unsparingly, Leighton thought. "I saw what they did in Germany. They bombed quite indiscriminately."

"I guess we did too," Willoughby grinned.

"That is not what I was told, young man." The senator turned on him.

"Well, you'll be quite safe and comfortable here at the Leightons', Senator," Snow smiled.

"Perhaps," said Bridgehorn, scanning the skies for the planes, "I should cable the Army — or the Navy. They must have plenty of idle planes out in this Godforsaken part of the world."

"I've been trying to get my good friend to do just

that." Groves spoke up, glancing triumphantly at Leighton. He had joined the gathering but a moment before.

"You didn't cable the Pentagon?" the senator asked Leighton.

"Our communications are confined to the State Department, Senator. I keep it informed daily. I have cabled it about your plight."

"And the answer, Leighton?" Bridgehorn pressed him.

"I expect we shall hear tomorrow, sir."

"Not from the Department. It never does anything unless — and until — the United States Senate forces it to."

"Come, Senator. It's not that bad," Leighton smiled.

"Don't get me started on that, Leighton," Bridgehorn roared. "Sometimes, I tell you, I feel like voting to abolish the damned thing. I certainly do my utmost to cut down the Department's appropriation. I've saved the taxpayers a few millions there, I can tell you."

"A cruiser, or even a couple of American destroyers, would clean up this situation here, Senator," Chester Groves said.

"Well, why haven't we sent for them?" Bridgehorn asked.

"Perhaps my good friend here can tell you that," Groves said, smiling maliciously at Leighton.

"The senator, I am sure," Leighton responded quietly, "knows our government policy on that better than I do."

"We're against meddling in these foreign wars, if that's what you mean!" Bridgehorn snorted.

"Even if we wanted to intervene, our British friends wouldn't accept it," Leighton added.

"Well, they seem to be in a hell of a mess. But perhaps you're right, Leighton. We should leave them to stew in it. Only, I say it is no place for a United States Senator. Besides, I have important work awaiting me back in Washington. I am wasting valuable time here."

"Didn't I read that Congress had adjourned?" Snow could not help blurting out.

"I mean I have important committee work, sir," the senator said, puffing.

Ilka Leighton said nothing. She too, in a dozen foreign posts, had acquired much experience of visiting Congressmen, and she had felt it wisest to keep her thoughts to herself and let Harold handle them. He had always done it admirably, too, she thought. He treated them most diplomatically, with respect and consideration, but he had never knuckled down to them as some of his more eager and ambitious colleagues had. Still, she thought, this preposterous man boded them no good. He would be one more burden for Harold and for her to bear in the next few difficult days. Groves, it was plain, would do his best to turn the senator against her husband. She would have to watch that.

In the meantime there was directly ahead of them the dinner this evening at Government House. Why had old Branhope invited them alone? What did he know? How should she act? Could she conceal what was boiling within her? Would Harold be able to bring the old tyrant around to reason? If so . . . ? . . . If not . . . ?

She waited impatiently for her guests around the tea table to clear out.

Chapter 11

JOHN LEE CAVENDISH, Viscount Branhope, too was nearing the end of a long career.

Musing in his study at Government House over a preliminary highball that evening just before the Leightons arrived, he was thinking that the way this strange, hurried world was going he, like a dwindling number of other Englishmen of his stripe, would soon be *arbeitslos*, as the Germans said — out of work. Soon there would not be any more governor-generalships nor many more governorships, except on a few stray forlorn islands here and there. Well, in three years he would be seventy, and it was time to retire.

He had had a pretty full life in the service of his country and he was fairly content with it. As soon as he put down this absurd rebellion — it had got out of hand before he realized it — he would negotiate with the decent and moderate elements in Pawancore for an eventual withdrawal and then relinquish this last of a dozen posts he had held in the once great Empire that he now recognized was fast crumbling into the dust of all the world empires of past time. Within a year or two he would be on his way back to England, this time for good. In fact, the principal reason for Lady Branhope's spending the summer in England was to arrange for renovating the ancestral home in Cornwall, which had fallen somewhat into a state of disrepair during the long years they had been away. In recent months he had thought a good deal of that home, the green and spacious lawns, the woods, the gardens. He would like nothing better than to spend a good part of his declining days puttering about in the garden and sprucing up the place.

There would be leisure too for writing. He was rather proud of the two-volume work he had turned out in his spare time some years back: *A History of British Rule in India. The Times* had reviewed it quite favorably and he had received a surprisingly large number of letters from home praising it. Only the Indian nationalist press had really disliked it. But of course that was to be expected. The non-British newspapers in India were too much taken in by Gandhi and Nehru to appreciate what British rule had done.

His London publisher had been pestering him the past year to do at least two new books: his memoirs, of course, which they wanted to call *Memoirs of a British Proconsul* — he wasn't sure he liked that title; and a book which he himself had suggested on how and why Britain was losing — with unnecessary speed, he thought — her great possessions in Asia, above all, India, that once sparkling jewel of the Empire. He would have a lot to say that would not be especially pleasing to the Labor government, which he was now serving loyally but with mounting misgivings.

Of course, old fogy that he might be, he tried to keep up with the changing times. He thought even Leighton would concede that. A Britisher of his stamp did not bear easily with most Americans. Their manners were difficult to comprehend; in fact, they were often offensive to a survivor of the old school. And Americans did seem to him to be shallow and superficial. But Leighton was an exception. He would have been a credit to the British diplomatic service in which Branhope had started as a young man. Wasn't the fact that Leighton, in the prime of his life, was only a consul-general in a backward Asian land, proof that he was an exception? Americans did not appreciate a cultivated and cultured man like that. They passed him by.

Not that he had always been pleased by the way Leighton threw his weight around, and the weight of the mighty United States, which overnight, so to speak, had become the foremost of the world powers. The consul-general had never let up on his pressure to hurry the British out of here. And he had tried to interfere, as he was doing at this very moment, whenever one tried to stem the tide momentarily with a little toughness. Most vexing of all was that Leighton argued eloquently that he had history behind him. And perhaps he did. No

Englishman of Branhope's traditions could fail to feel a little gall at seeing two non-British nations, America and Soviet Russia, emerge from the second war as the two principal powers on the planet. It did not fill him with pleasure to see Great Britain taking a back seat. He was bound to feel a sense of personal loss, of personal defeat, at the dreadful prospect of the dissolution of the Empire in whose service he had spent a strenuous life.

Yes, as Leighton kept harping, times were changing, though unlike his American friend, Branhope had strong doubts whether the changes were for the better. But an Englishman had to face the facts. A Labor government, the first with a clear Labor majority in the Commons in British history — and this fact itself was an ominous reminder of the drastic changes at home — was pulling out of India without a fight. Soon it would be getting out of Pawancore. The Dutch were finished in Indonesia. But unlike the British, they had been unable to hold their main possessions against the Japanese during the war. Branhope could understand — even if he didn't entirely agree — that the Americans, having reconquered the East Indies from the Japs, had no intention of handing them back, intact, and as they were before, to the Dutch. The Americans were no doubt sincere in their opposition to "colonialism." They could afford to be, since the U.S.A. was a continent. But even a man as intelligent and as grounded in history as Leighton seemed to forget that England and Holland were tiny specks of lands and that they therefore needed colonial empires in Asia to maintain their high standard of living at home.

France, with its better-balanced domestic economy and its clever policy of including a large slice of North Africa in its "metropolitan" area, didn't need an Asian empire. But though the British and Americans had wrested back Indochina from the Japanese, the French, who had lost it to them, apparently were determined to hold on to it. In this, they would surely fail. If the British could not hold India — and Pawancore — how could the French imagine they would cling to Indochina!

They were all finished, all of the European powers in Asia. Britain would strive to hold out for some time in Hong Kong, Singapore and Malaya. But Pawancore was to follow India. His job, so far as he understood it — London had told him to get the best settlement he could — was to prepare the way for an orderly transition to self-government for Pawancore within the Empire. Pawancore, lacking leaders like Gandhi, Nehru and Patel and the mass political party organization which they had built up in India, needed more time — at least two or three years. If he were to pull out tomorrow, there would be bloody chaos. The situation at the moment was bad enough. He hoped that Leighton would see that drastic measures, which he regretted as much as anyone, were now necessary and that the American consul-general would so inform his government.

He was sorry that Leighton was leaving. It would be too much to expect the Americans to replace him with a man of equal caliber. But it was a good thing for Mrs. Leighton that they were departing. Personally he had found this beautiful woman strange and fascinating. She reminded him of his younger days in the diplomatic service before he switched to the Colonial Office and the India Office. In half a dozen European capitals, especially in Budapest and Vienna, he remembered meeting women like her. They had always intrigued him.

Unfortunately, Mrs. Leighton had somehow got herself emotionally involved in this thing out here. It sometimes happened. In his fifteen happy years in India, as Governor of Bombay, as Governor of the Punjab, as a member of the Viceroy's Council, he had occasionally had to do with European or American women who became unduly sympathetic to the nationalists. Fortunately most of them were English and could be easily dealt with. There was that daughter of a famous British general who had become a member of Gandhi's household. He had had to arrest her, along with the rest. He still recalled the flaming headline in a London penny paper: *Lord Branhope Jails General's Daughter!*

But thank heaven! — none of them were wives of foreign consuls. And that raised a certain problem, which he was glad Leighton's departure would solve. He certainly did not want to become embroiled with the

United States of America in an unpleasant diplomatic incident! It would never do to arrest the wife of the American consul-general! And especially the wife of Harold Leighton, for whom he had such a high regard; and especially, too, such a beautiful and charming woman! He well knew that, next to Lady Stanhope, Mrs. Leighton was easily the most popular white woman in Pawancore City. He wished he knew exactly what she thought she was up to with that fanatical young Govind Singh. His C.I.D. was sure she was up to something. But since their meetings until his disappearance had been held mostly in the Leighton villa, where the C.I.D. had been unable to plant a trustworthy agent among the servants — Leighton, the shrewd devil, had foiled them on that, or perhaps it was Mrs. Leighton — the information was decidedly sketchy. He had thought it his painful duty to put the consul-general on guard. But Leighton quite naturally could not believe any ill of a woman with whom he was obviously still terribly in love and who, after all, was his wife. Perhaps he was right, at that. Half the reports of the C.I.D., on further investigation and checking, turned out to be little more than rumor.

Perhaps Mrs. Leighton, like a number of other European women in the capital, had simply been charmed by the handsome and dynamic young Sikh lawyer. He would give a pretty penny, incidentally, to know where the young man had absconded to. He had disappeared without a trace, making the C.I.D. look perfectly ridiculous, Branhope thought.

A knock on the door abruptly terminated his random thoughts. An aide announced that the Leightons had arrived.

The noble lord, Ilka saw at once, was at his most charming. He was, she had to admit, a striking-looking old man, tall, angular and with a rather beaked nose arching down from the strong gray eyes. He had an almost massive forehead that looked even more ample than it was because the top of the head into which it ran was bald and there was no telling where the two met. There were patches of white hair on each side above the large ears and a flowing pure-white mustache that half hid the thin lips. Lord Branhope reminded her of several old men of the Hungarian nobility — perhaps most of all of the indestructible Count Apponyi — whom she had seen in Budapest as a young girl, though the governor also had the stamp of the overbred English aristocracy, in which so many of the elder men she had met bore a close resemblance to each other, as if they were all hatched from the same nest. Lord Branhope spoke slowly, deliberately, as though there were nothing in the world that he had yet encountered which gave cause for undue hurry or worry. This was a quality which Ilka admired; did she not give that impression herself?

Lord Branhope greeted them warmly. "I am so sorry," he smiled, "that Lady Branhope is not here. She will never forgive herself for having been away at the moment of your going."

"Perhaps we can call on her in England if we go home that way," Leighton said.

"That would be splendid. She would so appreciate it, I know," Branhope beamed. He turned to Mrs. Leighton. "I must say I don't know how we're going to carry on out here when you and your husband are gone."

"You are most flattering, Lord Branhope," Ilka said, putting on her most glittering smile. This was the kind of mechanical diplomatic talk that she had learned from long experience to carry on as if by rote. It helped, too, she thought, to hide her uneasiness.

"I really mean it, every word of it," Branhope said. "It is a great personal loss, your departing like this."

"We are sorry to leave Pawancore," Leighton replied. "But, Governor, my five years were up. It was time to move on, you know."

"To greater opportunities, I know. What is it they're making you, Leighton?" Branhope spoke genially. "Assistant Secretary of State?"

"Good Lord, no!" Leighton laughed. "Assistant to the Secretary of State."

"One of those subtle distinctions of the State Department, eh?" Branhope said with a chuckle. "Well, whatever it is, Leighton, you more than deserve it. But I must say, my dear fellow, you will be irreplaceable out here. Whom are they sending out, by the way?"

"I haven't heard yet, Governor. But I am sure it will be someone much better than I."

"Impossible, Leighton! I would settle for someone half as good!"

"And half as troublesome, no?" Leighton said with a twinkle in his eye. Ilka, watching him, was relieved to see him in such relaxed spirits.

"We've had our differences, Leighton," Lord Branhope smiled, looking at the younger man benignly. "Good Lord, Leighton! How you've argued! But it has all been very helpful, I assure you. I shall miss all those long and involved discussions we had. I really shall, you know."

And with that he took Mrs. Leighton's arm, and led them into dinner.

But afterward, over coffee and brandy, the conversation took a more serious turn, as the Leightons had anticipated and desired. In fact Leighton deliberately provoked it. This would be his last opportunity to dissuade the old gentleman from embarking on a very foolhardy and reckless course. And he was glad that Ilka was there to hear him too. Somehow, judging by her strange moods in recent days, she had not seemed to understand fully what he was striving so desperately to accomplish. She had appeared to feel that he was letting events take their natural course. This had led, on top of his uneasiness over the other matter — the one the governor had raised — to an estrangement that baffled and hurt him.

He had asked for and this very day received from the Department its backing to inform Lord Branhope as forcibly as he could that any action on the part of the Government of Pawancore such as the threatened hanging of nationalist leaders would create a most painful impression on the American people.

"I therefore make this final appeal to you, sir," Leighton said gravely, after reading his brief message and expounding on it, "not to go ahead with these courts-martial and their fatal consequences."

"And may I add a woman's appeal to Your Excellency's humaneness?" Ilka said. She had been deeply moved by her husband's burning concern and his utter sincerity, but watching the governor-general as Harold spoke, she could see with a sickening heart the old man's face harden and turn to stone.

"Leighton — and Mrs. Leighton," Branhope said, and both of them caught for the first time a note of impatience, almost of exasperation, in his eyes and in his voice, "may I speak frankly?"

"Please, sir," Leighton said.

"I should like to go back a little, if I may. As I have often told my good friend, Mrs. Leighton," he said, glancing at her as if he especially wished her to follow his words closely, "I know perfectly well that we have to get out of here, as we are getting out of every place else in Asia except perhaps Hong Kong, Singapore and Malaya. But be assured of one thing. We are not going to surrender to force — and crawl out on our hands and knees!"

He paused and looked squarely at the other two.

"Leighton — and Mrs. Leighton — may I get something off my old British chest? Much of it will not be new to you, sir," he said, turning to Leighton. "A great deal of it possibly may never have occurred to you, Mrs. Leighton," he added, and though his voice was soft and kindly, Ilka felt his gray eyes stabbing at her . . . "preoccupied as you, the wife of a consul-general, invariably must have been with other matters.

"To begin with, I myself, obviously, have had nothing to do with our being here. That was an accident of history — and like so many others, you might say, without much rhyme or reason. Anyway, we came. To Asia. And we have stayed a couple of hundred years. No doubt, we committed many wrongs. Show me a conqueror who hasn't. No doubt, we made a lot of money out of these people, despite their appalling poverty. Perhaps we shouldn't have. But I am not responsible for the acquisitiveness of the white man in so many far corners of the earth; not only in Asia, but in Africa and in South America, and — not so long ago, if I may say so — in *North* America. You had your kind of Indians, and where are they now?

"On the other hand," Branhope continued, and Ilka

could not get over how mellow he sounded — mellow, gentle, tolerant — this strange man who in the same kindly mood would be signing tomorrow the death warrants of decent men, "on the other hand, we did a little good out here, I think — in India and in these dependencies such as Pawancore here. We found chaos; a breakdown of society; a hundred various peoples butchering each other. We established peace. We restored law and order. We did more. We built railways, highways, dams, canals, schools, hospitals. In quite a number of ways we improved the life — not of the few but of the many."

Lord Branhope paused and smiled. "Do I bore you?"

"On the contrary," Leighton said.

"Please go on," Ilka was surprised to hear herself mutter.

"We did something else that deserves mention. We began to educate these Asian people to democracy — something they had never known, as we know that term. Since democracy can only mean self-rule, wasn't that proof, given long ago, that we intended our stay out here to be limited in time, that we meant to let these peoples, as soon as they were able, govern themselves — and ourselves retire?

"We even encouraged them, as you know, to send their youth to England to complete their university education and to see how democracy worked at home. Men like Gandhi and Nehru in India, like this young Sikh fanatic Govind Singh here, took advantage of that. Such things were never done before by other conquerors, I believe. In sum, we nourished the seed that now has sprouted all over Asia and particularly in the places where we have ruled. The grain is now ripening. Do you think we don't see that — and are not prepared to act accordingly, that is to say: to get out? If not today, then certainly tomorrow?"

"Tomorrow can be — or seem — to these people a long way off," Ilka said. For the first time she began to see that Branhope, in the perspective of history, had a case, however much he exaggerated it, however much he overlooked.

"However long it may have seemed — or been — Mrs. Leighton," the governor replied, "it is here now. That is why I deeply regret all the bloodshed they are stirring up. It is futile, senseless."

"May I be equally frank with you, sir?" Leighton spoke up.

"You always are, Leighton."

Leighton tried to pick his words carefully. They had come to the crucial issue and it was one to which the governor — any colonial governor — paradoxically enough, was both blind and supersensitive.

"To be completely objective about it, Governor," Leighton proceeded, "your government's promises of self-rule go back rather far — twenty, thirty, forty years. Now, would it be entirely unreasonable for a Sikh or

Hindu here — let us try to put ourselves in their shoes for a moment — to conclude that those promises had been broken?"

"Postponed, Leighton, but not broken," Branhope quickly asserted.

No Englishman, a peer above all, Ilka thought, would ever admit that his word had been broken, though out here, as in India, it had been — time after time. The English, in this regard, were as hypocritical as the Germans. They had always reminded her of Prussian *Junkers*, who jabbered ceaselessly about their sense of honor but did the most dishonorable things. However, she said nothing. She did not want to jeopardize Harold's last desperate attempt to bring this man around to reason.

"It may have been difficult, Governor," Leighton said, breaking into a slight smile, "to always see the difference. However that may be, it leads us to what I have said before was the one important difference between you and the nationalist leaders here. That is the question of timing. Rightly or wrongly, sir, they distrust your promises. They want a definite date set for taking over. And I must say, sir, that I believe they are justified — if you will pardon my bluntness."

"Go ahead, Leighton," Branhope said.

"Therefore, if you will set a date — any reasonable date — one year, two years, even three years, the responsible men of the Nationalist Party will, in my opinion, certainly accept it. And your troubles, Governor," Leighton added with a smile, "will be over."

Ilka repressed an urge to reach over and embrace her husband. How had she ever doubted him, she who above all others knew the strength and the purity of his character? She turned anxiously to the governor.

"Leighton," he said, his face and voice imperturbable as before. "I have given a great deal of thought to all you have said over the past few weeks. There is much merit in your contention that we should set a definite date, though, as I have pointed out to you, this is a matter to be decided finally in London. But even if the Colonial Office concurred in establishing a date, certainly you, with all your long experience, can see that it is out of the question until this rebellion is put down. I think you will agree that I tried to be patient. I negotiated for our eventual withdrawal with an open mind and with complete sincerity. The answer they gave me was violence, war. If they want a trial of force, they shall have it. And for the past few months you have seen that they do want it.

"They have left me, therefore, Leighton, with no alternative. I must meet force with force. And we shall see," he smiled, "whose is the greatest."

Ilka could sense Leighton's spirits ebbing away; her own were crushed. "I am sorry to hear you say that, sir," Harold said earnestly.

"I shall tell you," Branhope resumed confidently, "for

the confidential information of your government, which has become so interested in the fate of this faraway country, what, after great soul-searching, believe me, Leighton, I have decided to do. As a matter of fact, I discussed it with you just the other evening. It is this.

"I now have the reinforcements to clean the rebels out of Pawancore City. We have been softening them up with some old bombers and tanks. On July fifth we shall begin a major operation. Within a week, I am confident, we shall utterly destroy them. The pacification of the upcountry will take more time. But I have been promised an infantry division from home in the fall for that."

"And the courts-martial?" Leighton asked.

"They are going ahead, Leighton. I believe the first verdicts will be in tomorrow, or the day after. I presume all the accused will be found guilty. The sentences, I should judge, will be pretty much automatic — under the law there can be only one sentence for treason. That is pretty general throughout the world, I believe."

"But, Your Excellency!" Ilka could not suppress a cry.

"Madame, you may be sure that I shall exercise clemency in a large number of cases. But not in all, I am afraid. I shall try to differentiate between the political leaders and those actually in charge of the fighting. For the latter and for the other terrorists I shall have to let the law take its course."

"As I told you, sir, when we first discussed it the other evening," Leighton said earnestly, "I consider such a course to be nothing less than cold-blooded murder."

"And I consider it to be, Leighton," Branhope answered, showing some heat for the first time, Ilka noted, "nothing less than justice. The law, Leighton, never murders. It administers justice."

What more was there to say? Leighton felt sunk in defeat. He had sought to the limit of his physical and mental powers, and had gone far beyond the proper functions of a foreign consul, to avert this disaster. He had failed. It remained only to face the failure with grace. Relief from the summer's mounting tension and his final frustration would come soon with their departure. He turned to Ilka to give a sign that he wanted to leave. She was gazing at Branhope, her eyes burning with hatred. Though protocol, he knew, called for the governor-general to indicate the end of the evening, Leighton rose to go.

"I hope we are still friends, despite all our differences," Branhope said, grasping Leighton's hand.

"Certainly, sir," Leighton said sadly.

"I shall miss you — both of you," Branhope added.

"We shall miss Pawancore," Leighton said. "It is a lovely land. We came to love it."

"Incidentally," Lord Branhope said, almost jokingly, "there is one nationalist fellow we haven't been able to get our hands on."

"Singh?" Leighton said.

"He flew the coop — left not a trace — most remarkable."

"He is a clever fellow," Leighton said.

"You wouldn't have any idea where we could put a finger on him, would you, Leighton?"

"No, sir," Harold said, unmindful that Ilka was holding her breath.

And then as they approached the door, Ilka remembered. Summoning all her strength to force a smile, she said: "Can we count on Your Excellency for the Fourth of July? It will be, I'm afraid, our farewell garden party."

"By all means, madame," Lord Branhope said, expansively. "I shall be looking forward to it."

Chapter 12

ALL THROUGH the third day of July, the tension in Pawancore City grew.

At ten A.M., the government radio announced the verdicts of the first courts-martial. In all five cases the accused were found guilty of treason and sentenced to death. In protest, the labor unions called an immediate general strike and at noon the Shopkeepers' Association declared a *hartal* and within an hour the shops and stores in the bazaars closed down.

In the dock area the fighting flared up. Shortly before noon Bob Snow, watching from the upper floor of the consulate, was surprised to hear the staccato bursts of machine guns from the old buildings where the guerillas were holding out. The nationalists must have smuggled in half a dozen of the weapons during the night, he surmised. By noon government tanks went into action to knock them out with their 75-millimeter guns and soon a wave of bombers flew over to help them.

Senator Bridgehorn was beside himself. He stormed into Leighton's office, his face purple and dripping with perspiration, his great jowls palpitating, and demanded succor. To quiet him, Leighton got off another urgent telegram to Delhi asking for the courier plane to come to the rescue. He called up the governor-general and suggested that he put a plane at the senator's disposal.

Bob Snow tried to help.

"We are really quite safe here and at the Leighton villa, Senator," he assured him. "In fact, I doubt very much whether we shall even suffer much inconvenience. Army engineers and personnel have taken over the water works and electric plants and also the telephone exchange. The only inconvenience is that the shops are closing."

"I don't want to shop. I want to get out of here!" Bridgehorn fumed.

"Maybe the plane will come today," Snow said.

"And maybe it won't! What do we have an Air Force for, I'd like to know!"

"Perhaps the governor can spare a plane." Leighton tried to calm the man.

"What did he say?"

"He said he would try to find one for you, sir."

They sent the senator back in a consulate car to the villa.

Snow himself thought it might be best to call off the Fourth of July garden party. "No one will come, Harold — with all this trouble," he said.

Leighton smiled: "Bob, you don't know the consular

[169]

set — and our English friends. They will come, all right. You will be surprised how little all this disturbs them."

"What about the local people, the Hindus and Sikhs?"

"They'll come too, quite a few of them — the office-holders, the office-seekers, the so-called moderates, who are hoping the governor will turn the place over to them some day. The nationalist crowd, of course — those who haven't been arrested or aren't out raising hell — will stay away, except for a spy or two. But we'll have a crowd, Bob." He scanned the skies, which were cloudless under the blazing sun. "I believe we're going to be lucky, Bob," he said.

"How, lucky?"

"The monsoon seems to be over."

Snow looked out. "By God, I believe it is."

Ilka Leighton too would not hear of calling off the garden party when Snow broached the matter at tea that afternoon. She seemed to him to be rather high-strung — but so was everyone else on this trying day. Moreover, she must have a dozen details to worry over in connection with arranging the Fourth of July reception. The kitchen, he gathered, was humming, and every few moments Ilka left the tea table on the terrace to hurry down to the garden to direct the servants who were erecting a marquee, arranging tables and chairs and flowers, and manicuring the lawn and the hedges.

"We couldn't disappoint so many people," Ilka said to Snow. "Besides," she smiled, glancing at the unhappy

Bridgehorn, "as the senator was saying a moment ago, we have to honor the Fourth."

"The Fourth of July is a glorious day for Americans," Bridgehorn declared, his voice rising in sonorous tones. "It must be observed, in all circumstances. If I am here tomorrow, as I begin to suspect I shall be," he added, glancing malevolently at Leighton, "I shall certainly join in the celebration with all my heart."

"By this time tomorrow, Senator, you should be in Delhi," Leighton said, "But if you are not, if you are still here, we shall be honored by your presence, sir."

"Personally, Senator, I should resent your leaving us on the eve of the garden party." Ilka backed up her husband with the most gracious of smiles. She was beginning to wonder, though, whether the old windbag might not complicate matters. In fact, she hoped a plane — any plane — would arrive in time to take him away.

She had been crushed as she listened to the ten A.M. bulletin on the government radio. As soon as she had recovered from the shock, she had gone out to the garden to tell Singh. There were two or three other servants about, helping to put up the marquee and arranging the garden furniture, and it took some mutual maneuvering before they could get apart for a word.

Singh was not surprised at her news. "Just as I told you, madame," he said. In fact, he seemed to her to be relieved. "Nothing is to prevent us now from going ahead," he said.

[171]

"But Singh!" Ilka cried. "The governor will surely commute the sentences. He told us last night he would."

"All of them?" Singh asked sharply.

Ilka returned his glance with the same sharpness. It would be best for the moment to evade him, she thought. But she could not bring herself to do it.

"No . . . He didn't say . . . all of them," she faltered.

"Even if he does commute all of them, he will have to act quickly. If there is any doubt about it by tomorrow, we shall go ahead."

Time was running out on her. She could not, she sensed, vacillate much longer. If only she had the power of decision of this brave young man! For or against. Do or not do. But she knew she didn't have it. The old feeling of terror began to grip her.

"You promised you would do nothing . . . unless . . ." she started to say.

"Unless what?" he asked calmly.

". . . Unless . . . there were actual executions."

"My good friend," Singh said, "tomorrow is our only chance. We cannot wait."

"Murder will accomplish nothing, Singh," Ilka said desperately.

"It will answer murder. It will revenge it. It will be simple justice."

"My husband . . . last night . . . called them that," Ilka murmured.

"The hangings?"

"Yes . . . He told the governor to his face . . . He said . . . they would be cold-blooded murder . . . Harold was so wonderful . . . so courageous . . ."

"And he was right," Singh said.

"Yes." Ilka looked away.

"You have not yet told me, madame," Singh said, "what the governor said last evening."

"It is academic now, my friend," Ilka replied, "after this bulletin on the radio."

"Did he discuss anything else?" Singh persisted.

Ilka hesitated, debating with herself. "Yes," she finally replied, "but I don't think I should tell you. It would be rather treasonous."

Singh broke into a smile. "You are one of us, you know."

"Am I?" Ilka said slowly. That was what was so hard to face. Had she really become one of them? Had she any right to?

"We count you so," Singh said simply.

"Well," Ilka said. At least on this point she would make a clear-cut decision. "He did mention his military plans."

"I would be interested to hear them."

"What can you do about them — cut off here?"

"I am not so cut off as you think."

"They're beginning a big operation, he said, on the fifth."

"The day after tomorrow."

"Yes."

"In the dock area?"

"Yes. He said it might take a week — to wipe out your people there."

"I am certainly obliged to you for letting me know," Singh said.

"What can you do about it?" Ilka had tried to clear her conscience with the thought that Singh could not possibly do anything about it. She had not really meant, she told herself uneasily, to betray the governor, however much she despised him.

"I think I can get it to our people within an hour," Singh said.

"How, may I ask?" Ilka said, taken back.

"I never told you," Singh smiled. "The consul-general's chauffeur is one of ours."

"I think you might have told me, Singh," Ilka said. They had been together in the garden much too long, she thought, and she moved to go.

"One more thing," Singh said. "Have you arranged for me to lug about a tray with the glasses of champagne tomorrow?"

"Not yet. Do you want to carry champagne?"

"You remember what I told you!"

Ilka remembered, but she did not say so. And now Singh was all nerves, she saw.

"This may be our last chance to go over it," he said,

his words tumbling out rapidly, the black pupils of his eyes dilating, "so there is no mistake! I will be carrying the champagne. You will get the old man aside. Take him by the arm and lead him toward the veranda and then into the living room. I have thought of your pretext."

"What!"

"The old boy knows you don't like him."

"How did you know?"

"You told me, for one thing."

"I suppose it's true," Ilka said.

"Now, here's the pretext. I have worked it out. You tell him you want to have a word with him — alone. Inside, where it is not so hot. And where it is quieter. You will soon be departing, you say, and you do not want to leave behind a misunderstanding. You realize, you say, that you have misunderstood him, and that perhaps he has not understood you. You want to clear this up. And so on. By this time, you have entered the living room. Ask him to sit down beside you. Talk earnestly to him about your misunderstanding. Tell him that especially after last night you see better his many problems —"

"As a matter of fact, I do," Ilka interrupted.

"All the better, then. You can be more sincere."

"Singh, no lies between us, please," Ilka said.

"All right. Sincere or not, praise him! Say how much Lady Branhope has meant to you!"

"That old bitch!" Ilka exclaimed.

[175]

"All right. We know she is. But you've been saying silly things all your life as the wife of a diplomat, haven't you? It will be easy for you. Now — finally! This, above all, remember, I pray you, madame. You make up with the old codger. And you propose a parting toast to your friendship. I shall be watching from a crack in the door to the dining room. You make a sign . . ."

"What sign?"

"I have figured that out too. You grasp his hands. That is the signal! I come in with a tray of the champagne glasses on my shoulder, as if I were merely passing on my way to the garden —"

"You will be too excited," Ilka broke in. "You will surely drop the tray!"

"This is no moment for pleasantries, madame — if you will pardon me. Now listen carefully, please. This is most important. Everything depends on it. You call out to me. You propose to the old man a toast with champagne. I come towards you. You jump up to take the two glasses. You must be careful to stand well aside. That is most important of all. You stand well aside! Don't get between us! In a second, then, it will be over!"

Chapter 13

THROUGH the bedroom window, Harold Leighton watched the sun break over the horizon beyond the bay, lighting up the green hills that ran up from the sea toward the villa. There was not a sign of a cloud and soon, he knew, the pink sky would turn to blue and then pale under the merciless sun. Well, at least, he said to himself, we will not be rained out this Fourth of July. The monsoon — there was no doubt of it — was spent.

He had not slept since midnight. The clammy heat was insufferable, but it was not that which had kept him awake. He glanced over at Ilka. She had finally gone to sleep. She lay on her bed under a thin sheet breathing irregularly, at times almost gasping for breath, and tossing from one side to the other.

He could not stand this much longer. Her nightmare had kept him up. Or was it a nightmare?

He had awakened during the night and found her bed empty. He had bounded out of bed and first raced to the bathroom. She was not there. He had rushed downstairs. There in the eerie light that the waning moon made, she was pacing up and down the living room in her flimsy white nightgown. She seemed in a trance. She did not, at first, appear to recognize him.

"My darling Ilka, what is the matter!" he had cried, rushing up to her, but she did not seem to hear. She brushed past him. She was murmuring incoherently; he could catch only a few words here and there.

. . . A terrible . . . misunderstanding, sir . . . All my fault . . . Let us be friends . . . I understand you better now . . . Your duty I know . . . I can't go on! . . . What! . . . I mean, look over at that crack in the door, kind sir! . . . No! No! Do not look! . . . Friends! . . . Friendship! . . . That is the important thing! . . . What am I saying! . . . Ah, yes. We will toast it in . . . in champagne! . . . In golden, sparkling champagne from la France! . . . Boy! Come here! . . .

She seemed to be crying out to him. "Boy! Come here!"

"Ilka! It is I! Harold!" he had shouted, taking her hands, and pulling her toward him. "You've been walking in your sleep, my dear. Wake up!"

He thought she had awakened. Her wild eyes stared at him. She was shuddering.

"You are Harold! . . . My husband! . . . My good husband! . . ." She had grasped him, still terror-stricken. "Take me away, then! . . . Out of this room,

Harold! . . . Away from this bloody place! . . . This minute! . . . This minute, my love, or we are lost! . . ."

"Darling, please!" he had exhorted her, but she had ranted on. In the diffused, silvery light the white of her eyeballs stood out as if there were no pupils left, as if the whole of her eyes had turned a ghastly white.

She tugged at him. "We will go out this door, my darling . . . over the veranda . . . into the garden . . . down the road . . . and set sail . . . and never be seen here again . . ."

"Ilka, please!"

"Shall we do it, my love! . . . While there still is time! . . . Have you the courage! . . . The imagination! . . . Oh God, Harold! . . . Please! . . . Save us! . . . Save us both! . . . Take me away! . . ."

"I will take you away, my love," he had said, and had gently guided her, her body throbbing with convulsions, out through the veranda and around the garden and back, and then he had led her carefully upstairs and placed her on her bed, where she had sunk back in uneasy sleep.

What was it all about? he wondered. Poor, darling, beautiful Ilka — the strain of these last days was telling on her at last, on her who had always had such strength to keep her emotions hidden even from him. He sat on the edge of his bed watching her. She seemed to be asleep. Had he really awakened her? The words she had mumbled made no sense. What was it, though, that was so troubling her?

She had been desolated, he remembered, by the governor's words the evening before last, so numbed by them in fact that she had not spoken a word to him in the car coming home. Then, as they talked it over before going to bed that night, her gloom had turned to bitterness and she had finally exploded in a violent outburst against Lord Branhope.

"He ought to be struck down for such a hideous crime!" she had fumed.

The announcement yesterday of the courts-martial verdicts had again plunged her into despondency. But somehow, he had noticed, perhaps because she had had to turn her mind to the preparations for the garden party, she had seemed to recover her spirits. She had even been amiable with the inimitable senator, who was proving so vexing to everyone else.

Leighton looked over again at his wife. She seemed to be breathing a little easier. He hoped she would have the strength to get through this trying day. She had great endurance and a very hard core within her. If she could get a few hours of sleep now she would no doubt be her old self for the rest of the day. The garden party would be a terrible bore for both of them. But at least they would be sustained by the pleasant thought that it was the last such affair they would be having here — in fact, the last they probably would ever have. In Washington they would be much too small fry to have to entertain very much. By God, Washington in the autumn! Perhaps they could grab a week or two off to drive through New England and feel the cool, clear, bracing air there and see the riotous colors of the turning maple leaves. That was something to look forward to! With such thoughts he dozed away for an hour or two.

Ilka came down to breakfast just as they were about to tune in on the ten o'clock news. To Leighton's joy and relief, she looked refreshed — in fact she seemed so buoyant, so much her vital old self that Leighton wondered for a moment if last night's nightmare had not been his. Perhaps, he chuckled to himself, it was he who had had the bad dream.

She greeted everyone warmly and apologized for being late.

"I simply overslept," she smiled.

"Madame, it is a holiday," Senator Bridgehorn said. "It is the thing to do. Despite the cursed heat, I slept late myself."

"I am happy that you will be with us today, Senator," Ilka responded amiably.

"I shall make the best of necessity, dear madame. I shall be glad to help you celebrate this glorious day!"

"As a matter of fact, Senator, it sort of sounds like the Fourth of July at home, doesn't it — at least in the old days," Bob Snow teased him. They could hear considerable rifle fire from the direction of the port and occasionally the deeper and louder roar of a 75-millimeter shell exploding.

"Those are not firecrackers, I believe," the senator said, sitting up and cocking an ear.

"Right," said Snow.

Isobel got up and turned on the radio. A hush came over the table. A Hindu announcer with a Hinduized Oxford accent read a special announcement from Government House. Leighton's face fell. He saw Ilka's eyes flash, her cheeks fill with color. The announcer's voice was matter-of-fact. The death sentences of two of the five persons found guilty by courts-martial had been graciously commuted to life imprisonment at hard labor by His Excellency the Governor-General. Because two of the others had been captured while actually leading an armed rebellion against His Majesty's forces and a third had confessed to acts of sabotage and murder, His Excellency the Governor-General had found no reason to interfere with the carrying out of their sentences. The three men — no one at the table caught their names — were hanged at dawn this morning in the Central Prison . . .

"I didn't believe he would do it," Snow said sadly.

"Just a minute — there's something more," Leighton said, glaring intently at the little radio box.

The governor-general, the voice said, had delivered this morning a final ultimatum to the armed rebels in the dock area. He called upon them to surrender by sunset this fourth of July. If they did not, they would be attacked at dawn on July fifth, in overwhelming force by His Majesty's troops, warships and planes, and utterly destroyed.

So that was that, Leighton thought, a great deadness spreading through him. The big attack was to be expected and in the circumstances was justified, though it would be a terrible slaughter. He had never argued with Branhope over that. But the other thing — well, there was nothing he could do about it now. And he must hide his feelings when the governor came this afternoon. He looked at Ilka. She was staring at her half-eaten dish of cereal, her black eyes watering, the muscles in her neck throbbing; she was struggling, he could see, to retain a grip on herself.

"I must say," the senator said, "the governor appears to be acting with great energy. But how else can you put down a rebellion?"

"By other means than hangings, sir," Snow said coolly.

"I must say, I don't like that either. Was it necessary?"

"No, Senator," Leighton said. "I told the governor a thousand times it was not necessary, nor, in my opinion, justified. It will inflame the country. These people are human, like any others."

"Well, sir, I hope you will get me out of here before it stirs up the country any further."

"I shall keep on trying, Senator." Leighton smiled wanly.

He regretted that he and Snow had agreed to play golf this morning with the senator and Chester Groves at the country club. It was outlandish that country clubs should function at a moment of tragedy and death like this. But somehow they always did. In how many moments of crisis in how many capitals when men were dying in war or bombings or uprisings or bloody purges had he been outraged at the sight of men, especially the foreign diplomats and the well-heeled natives, continuing to play their rounds of golf at the swank clubs, as if these places were a privileged world apart. Well, they were. They had no connection with the rest of humanity, with the ugliness of its existence, with its sufferings, its death pains. "Outraged" was an exaggeration all right, he smiled to himself. He had been outraged, had he? Then why so often at the most untimely moments had he participated in this game in these pleasant green places, and why was he about to do so this very morning when the tortured city lay writhing in its agony? For that matter, why were they giving a gala garden party on such a day? Perhaps Snow was right — they should have called it off.

He tried to beg off from the golf. "I'm afraid, Senator, Mrs. Leighton will need me here this morning."

"You run along with the others," Ilka said. "It will do you good, my dear." She really meant it, she told herself, Harold needed an outing after his illness and the pressures of the past few weeks. But also, God knew, she was afraid now — for the next few hours — to face him alone. What had she done last night? How much had she babbled! From this moment until late this afternoon she must struggle to reach her decision — alone. And if it should be what she now felt it must be, she would have to avoid giving herself away to him.

When they had gone — she had had to talk Isobel into keeping her engagement at the country club to play tennis with that young vice-consul, Willoughby — she went swiftly to the garden to find Singh.

He was not there. Or had he disguised himself so well that she could not recognize him? All the servants were in their dress livery, bulging white trousers, long red coats and flowing white turbans. She waited for Singh to come up and identify himself. She wanted to tell him . . . what? The hangings had helped her make up her mind. They would go ahead. As Singh would say, it was only elementary justice . . . If she could be sure she would not falter . . . He would strengthen her resolve . . .

Ilka inspected the marquee, the tables and chairs, the flowers, the state of the lawn and the hedges. All were in good order. She lingered, chatting to one servant and then another in Hindustani. Singh did not come up to her, as he had all the other times. Suddenly a feeling of terror seized her. He had been found during the night! Arrested! Some servant had finally recognized him and reported him. She and Harold had done their best to keep the C.I.D. from planting an agent among the help. One must have slipped in. Or an old trusted one had betrayed him!

She hurried to the kitchen. Singh worked part of the time there. He was not in the kitchen. She questioned the head cook. Was everything going smoothly?

"Yes, mem-sah'b," the heavily bearded first cook looked up from his pots and pans to say. "Here, all right. But in city, very bad!"

Ilka felt relieved, though not entirely. If there had been an arrest, the kitchen would be buzzing. And of course, the servants would have told her. Thank God, *that* hadn't happened! But what had? She did not dare question the servants more specifically. She checked with the first cook about the various items of food, and with the steward about the beverages and ice. There had been a power failure during the night, but the ice machine was working again. Everything in the kitchen was in order, she satisfied herself, and she departed for the garden once more.

The servants were idling about in the marquee to keep out of the broiling sun. Singh was not among them. Had he perhaps slipped away on his own? Had he been alerted that his hiding place had been found out? Surely he would have let her know. But how? A note would have been too dangerous. He might have asked a servant to tell her. Or would that have been too risky? Ilka stabbed in her mind frantically for an explanation. Singh couldn't have lost heart. He was much too brave and dedicated and single-minded for that. Besides, the news that morning of the executions would have cemented his resolution — as it had hers . . . had it not? Could it be, the thought came to her, that the news indeed had made final his resolve but . . . but that he did not quite trust her own? And that therefore he was avoiding her so as not to give her a chance to weaken, to argue, to vacillate and finally to welsh. Perhaps he was sure that some inner compulsion in her would carry her through the afternoon as he had planned it and that to discuss anything now might prove fatal. How little he knew!

The next few hours were a misery for Ilka. About one o'clock she tried to nibble a sandwich and sip a glass of chilled wine to give herself strength, but she had neither appetite nor — strangely, she thought, considering the oppressive heat and the fever that was burning inside her — thirst. At two-thirty, the others would be returning from the country club; the first guests would start arriving at four. She decided to take a shower and then change into her afternoon dress. When she came down to the living room at two-fifteen — she remembered afterward how she had glanced at her watch constantly all through that afternoon — a servant was

[187]

lazily dusting the bookcase which lined one side of the room. She sat down to smoke a cigarette and collect herself. The others would be along any minute now.

Actually, she felt in a feverish stupor and she told herself, biting her lips between the rapid cigarette puffs, that she must somehow shake it. Whatever happened she must have a clear, cold mind. The fever that was burning her up was purely mental — she must get rid of it. She must regain the strength, the hard outer shell, that had never failed her before in a crisis, in all her life. She had let Singh's disappearance exacerbate her already frayed nerves. She ought to see that his going had delivered her — perhaps that was why he had gone: out of his deep consideration for her and, yes, out of his deep love, for all along she had known that he loved her from his very depths. And she him? No . . . Not quite that . . . Something else . . . Much else . . . But this was no time to go over that again. He was gone. And the terrible nightmare was lifting. This would turn out after all to be just another dull Fourth of July garden party to go through with and, thank God! it was the last — the very last. A feeling of relief, of release, began to swell in her. She had been rescued — no matter if through no act of her own — from the supreme folly of her life.

She looked at her watch and listened for the sound of Harold's car coming up the driveway. She lit another cigarette. The servant, she had noticed with increasing annoyance, kept dabbing at the books with his dustcloth, his back turned toward her. He was taking a long time. He ought to be out with the others in the kitchen or the garden. It was time they were spreading the tablecloths and getting the plates and the silver out and the tables set. They were a good sort, these Pawancore servants, but they were lazy and dilatory.

Finally she called out rather sharply: "Why don't you go out to the garden where you're needed? You've dusted those books quite enough!"

"Yes, mem-sah'b," the man mumbled, without budging.

"Besides," Ilka added good-naturedly, "you're getting your coat all dusty." She herself had seen to it that all the liveries were freshly cleaned and pressed.

"Yes, mem-sah'b." He turned slowly and bowed low.

"Get along to the garden," Ilka said, and looked away. In the flush of her feeling of deliverance she really did not much care whether the lazy lout ever got a move on. She had not even bothered to notice which one of the dozen servants it might be. She glanced back to see. He was unbending, raising his head, his black-bearded face breaking into a broad and — it seemed to her for an instant — insolent grin. She stared at him.

"Your obedient servant, madame!" he said.

"My God!" At the sound of his natural voice Ilka shrieked.

"I am not too easily recognizable?" Singh smiled.

Ilka continued to gape at him. "Only your voice," she finally said. His own mother, she thought, would never recognize him in that garb and with that long silky black beard tied to his false mat of hair under the flowing turban.

"I can change the voice. And chatter like a silly servant. Shall I show you?" Singh seemed to Ilka to be in a peculiarly frivolous state of mind.

"Please don't," she said. "This is no time for levity, as you remarked to me a day or two ago." She felt numb still from the shock. "Were you here this morning," she said after a bit, "hiding behind that disguise and mocking me?"

"No. I . . ."

"I looked for you, you know."

"I had an errand," Singh said . . . "in the city."

"Errand?"

"I had to get this," Singh said, pressing one hand against a bulge that showed slightly from his inside pocket. "The old one — it was not entirely trustworthy. This one is." He patted the bulge. "We tested it just two hours ago."

"You must have been out of your mind, risking being discovered in town."

"It was a risk I had to take. But as you see, my make-up is not bad." Again Singh broke into a smile. His great beard gave it a somewhat grotesque effect, Ilka thought.

"You heard the news this morning?" she asked.

"Yes. It makes it easy for us now, doesn't it," Singh said quietly.

"I don't know. I feel terribly confused. I thought you had gone away."

"We can feel completely justified now, both of us," Singh said.

"Speak for yourself!" All the old doubts had returned to plague her.

"It is no longer a question of an evil deed, a crime — but of simple justice."

"Delude yourself, Singh. But not me, I beg you. To kill . . . to murder . . . is a crime."

"It is better not to discuss it further, I think," Singh said. "You will do your part, and I will do mine."

"I won't have the strength, Singh! Let's face it!"

"You will, though. I am confident."

"I haven't even arranged for you," Ilka hesitated . . . "to carry the champagne. I forgot . . ."

"Do not worry about that," Singh said. "I have arranged that myself — with your good people in the kitchen."

There was the sound of a door slamming shut in a car just off the veranda. Ilka saw that she had been too absorbed to hear Harold and his guests come up the driveway. They were mounting the steps of the veranda.

"You'd better hurry!" she whispered to Singh.

But as he started to go, two inspectors of the C.I.D. in white uniforms and carrying white topis in their hands came through the open doors of the veranda, led by Ilka's panting and frightened Hindu doorman.

"Madame, the gentlemen from the police!" the doorman blurted out.

Ilka sat frozen to the divan. She felt too paralyzed to move. Singh started to ease himself out of the room, flicking his dustcloth at the books and side-stepping softly toward the door to the dining room.

"Just a minute, young man!" One of the inspectors stopped him. The other approached Ilka.

"Excuse us, madame, for intruding. A routine inspection from the C.I.D. before His Excellency arrives. We arranged it with the consul-general yesterday."

"He did not tell me," Ilka managed to say.

"We will not disturb you, madame. It will take only a moment."

They both showed her their identity cards. Out of the corner of her eyes Ilka could catch Singh moving slowly, silently, on bare feet toward the door. My God! — if he had only left ten seconds sooner!

"Just a minute, boy!" One of the officers turned and strode up to Singh. Ilka felt her heart stop beating. This was the end! They had caught Singh red-handed — prowling around — with a revolver in his pocket in the very spot where in an hour or two the governor would be arriving! Ilka sank against the back of the divan and closed her eyes. They could take her too. She would not let them make away with Singh and herself remain silent. She would tell them . . .

"What's your name?" she heard the inspector ask gruffly.

"Janji Singh, sah'b." The voice was a mere squeak.

"How long you been here?"

"Five years, sah'b."

Ilka looked up. To her amazement, Singh seemed quite calm and sure of himself. He was properly respectful and he was answering in Hindustani in a high, almost falsetto voice with the peasant accent of the north country which he had often exhibited for her. But when they searched him! She braced herself for the catastrophe.

The inspector looked over at Ilka. "He's been with you a long time?"

She made a superhuman effort to answer, to give sound to her voice, to utter words. "Yes . . . From . . . the beginning . . . officer . . ." She tried to look away. She could not bear to see. Yet . . . She could not budge her eyes. They seemed glued to the corner by the door where the two men stood. She saw the inspector feel nimbly over Singh's trousers and then upward over his coat.

"Just a routine inspection, madame," he called over to her, grinning as he frisked Singh's pockets. Ilka could not breathe. The monster was playing with Singh like a cat with a mouse. Why did he prolong the agony!

And then, after an age, it was over.

"Okay, fellow. Carry on," the inspector said, slapping Singh on the back.

Ilka stared at them, still rigid with a feeling of paralysis. Her eyes sought the bulge which Singh had shown her on his coat a moment before. It was gone. How? — in God's name!

"Madame." The inspector moved toward her. "Are there any extra servants for this occasion?"

"No," Ilka said. She felt as if a load the size of a mountain had slipped off her. "We're getting along with what we have today."

"That relieves us somewhat," the officer grinned. "It's those extra ones people hire that we're particularly interested in."

The other officer, who had been giving the room a cursory inspection, glancing under the chair covers and behind the pictures and curtains, spoke up. "Roger, will you take a quick look in the kitchen and the servants' quarters? In the meantime I shall have a look upstairs." He turned to Ilka. "Have you any house guests, madame?"

"Yes," Ilka said. The sense of relief was soothing; she was managing to get her voice down to normal. "Mr. Snow, whom you know. And Senator Bridgehorn."

"Could you show me their rooms? It's all very routine, you understand, madame." The inspector smiled.

Despite her tension, Ilka could not help but smile to

herself as she watched the officer flick through the senator's two large suitcases. One was piled high with soiled crumpled shirts. The senator was certainly of the perspiring kind. She wondered why he had not given her the shirts for the laundry.

"Quite a reader, your senator," the Inspector chuckled, his nimble fingers turning up a half dozen books at the bottom of the bag. Ilka could not resist the temptation to look at their titles. On top was a book of Demosthenes' orations. Underneath a similar book of Cicero's orations. Underneath that a book on *The Love Life of the Bees*. She hadn't suspected that side of the eminent statesman, she mused.

Ilka accompanied the inspector downstairs to the living room. Singh was still puttering about with his dustcloth. Perhaps for the moment, now that he had been cleared, it was the safest spot. The other officer emerged from the kitchen.

"A frightfully clean and shining kitchen, madame," he greeted Ilka. "Is that the way they are in America?"

"Yes. Everything at home is supposed to be clean and shining," Ilka said. She was surprised — and relieved — to find herself almost smiling.

"Never saw so many gadgets and contraptions in my life!"

"I trust, Roger," the second officer said to him, "that you did not give in to your inclination to tinker with them."

"It was a temptation, sir. Never saw anything like it."

"Madame, you were very considerate." The first officer addressed Ilka. "If you don't mind, we shall now take a look at the garden. That's where the festivities take place, is it not?"

"That's right. Shall I come with you?" Ilka asked.

"It will not be necessary, madame."

As soon as they were gone, Ilka rushed breathlessly toward Singh.

"What happened! . . . I thought it was the end!"

"So did I — for a moment."

"What did you do . . . with the thing?"

Singh smiled. "I didn't have any choice — or much time. I stuck it back here."

He reached behind a row of books and took the shining Mauser automatic, glanced at it fondly, held it up to show to Ilka, and then slowly put it in his inside coat pocket. Then they heard the sound of Harold's car grinding up the graveled driveway.

"We shall meet here — once more," Singh said, his voice lowering almost to a whisper.

"Singh, I can't . . . I won't be able! No!" she cried.

But Singh had turned and without a glance backward, without listening, without a further word, he slipped through the door that led through the dining room to the kitchen.

Chapter 14

To THE SURPRISE of the Leightons, Lord Branhope, casting protocol to the winds, arrived a few minutes before four o'clock.

They had just completed a tour of inspection of the gardens and at Harold's suggestion had sat down in the living room to have a quiet smoke and a fortifying highball before the guests began to arrive. Ilka, Leighton could see, was a little high-strung, but then that was natural just before a big party. He felt a touch of guilt at having left all the work of preparation to her. It had been very wearing and she was obviously tired. Yet he could sense her pulling herself together, as she always did on such occasions. She had a remarkably good color in her face, and her eyes, which — no doubt from fatigue — had seemed a little expressionless a few minutes before, were beginning to brighten up and glisten. They were chuckling now over the senator's outburst an hour or so ago, when on his return Ilka had told him of the visit of the two inspectors from the C.I.D. The inspection had annoyed Leighton; though it was customary, he did not remember being told of it this time in advance. It had caused the senator to explode.

"You mean they had the effrontery to go through my personal effects!" he had roared.

"Before my very eyes," Ilka had confirmed it.

"Do they take me for a . . . for a confounded rebel!" Bridgehorn had fumed. "Am I to be treated in this God-forsaken land like a would-be assassin!"

"The old boy was really steamed up," Leighton laughed.

And he laughed again when Ilka, now, told him of the books the inspector had turned up in the senator's suit-case.

"The love life of the bees! I must ask him about it," Leighton chuckled.

"Somehow you don't associate the old windbag with that," Ilka said.

"Hardly," Harold said, checking his mirth.

Ilka was glad to see him in such good spirits. She envied him. It was obvious, she thought, that whatever his previous misgivings concerning her, he had now put them out of his mind. She could not detect the faintest hint of suspicion in his eyes or manner. God! She could never betray this decent, kindly man who still, despite all the years of familiarity, worshiped her. But was there any going back now? She had been gripped by the thought that she would not have the strength to go through with what Singh was intent on. But had she the strength — the iron in her veins — to *resist* going through with it now? Was there not some inner compulsion — indefinable but compounded of Singh's influence and her own independent reaction to what had happened here and in so many other turbulent places — that would sweep her on, like a leaf on the crest of a swollen torrent against which it was now too late to struggle? Or was there still free choice? God! She no longer knew! She would simply have to endure through the afternoon and let God, or Whoever presided over one's destiny — and some Being did, she was sure — lead her on — one way or the other.

Amidst these thoughts, and while with the outer crust of her mind she was conversing calmly with her husband, the doorman had entered and to their surprise announced the arrival of His Excellency.

"I hope you don't mind," Lord Branhope greeted them — "my coming a little early. I did want a quiet word with you before all those people arrive."

"You are most welcome, Governor," Leighton said.

Despite the heat, Ilka observed, the old man was attired in a formal cutaway coat and striped trousers, and carried a gray stovepipe hat in his hands.

"I just cannot get used to the idea of your leaving," Branhope went on. "I know I've said it before, and I don't want to sound tiresome, but I really feel strongly about it, you know. You leave such a void — both of you."

Ilka smiled, but she did not say anything. He was certainly a polished old gentleman, she was thinking. How could he be so cold and brutal deep down?

"You are looking your most beautiful today, madame," the governor beamed. However scatterbrained she might be about affairs here, he was thinking, and whatever the reasons for her curious hostility toward him, she was without doubt, he had to admit, the most stunning-looking woman in the foreign colony. There was certainly no one he could think of who could begin to replace her.

"You are most flattering, Your Excellency," Ilka smiled. She must imprint that smile on her face, she thought, for the rest of this dreadful afternoon and wear it like a mask.

"It is only the truth, my dear Mrs. Leighton," he responded. "By the way," he said, "I cabled Lady Branhope after our dinner the other evening. I have just had a reply. She is despondent, she says, at your going. But she hopes you can be her guests for a fortnight in September, if, as you mentioned the other evening, you should be going home by way of England. How does that fit into your plans?"

"Very well, thank you," Leighton answered. "We are planning to leave by the end of the month — I think my successor will be named by then. Bob Snow has talked us into taking a month's holiday in Europe — in the

Tyrol, where all three of us used to ski when we were young."

Ilka looked up. In the excitement she had forgotten that. But now she remembered that she herself had assented to Bob's entreaties that they all take a month off in the Tyrol. It seemed a haunting dream. But most probably she would never again see those lovely mountains below Innsbruck where her life with Harold had first blossomed.

"And then you might be going on to England, and sailing from there?" Branhope asked eagerly.

"That would be the thing to do," Leighton assented.

"Splendid! I shall cable Lady Branhope this very evening that she can count on you."

How strange, Ilka thought, that his man's mind could dwell on the trivial at such a moment. She would wager that he had eaten a hearty breakfast before the bodies of the three Hindus he hanged this morning were cold. No doubt tomorrow morning, when the slaughter of the big bombing and bombardment started down by the docks, he would do the same. And as for their visiting Lady Branhope in her musty old castle — if she, Ilka, should ever be free again to visit anybody — it was out of the question! That ugly old battle-axe, as some of the irreverent younger men at the consulate had called her! Ilka had always found it difficult to be civil to her.

"I suppose in a way, Mrs. Leighton" — Lord Branhope turned to her — "you feel relieved at the prospect of getting back to civilization."

"I don't know," Ilka said. Was the old man beginning to read her thoughts? Was her face so transparent? Harold and Bob Snow had always taunted her about its being so sphinxlike. "We both love Washington very much," she went on. "After all it is home, even though we've scarcely lived there."

"Like London to us," the governor chimed in.

"But we've liked it here too," Ilka added. "It has been very interesting."

"Still, it's a bit on the primitive side, I know," Branhope said.

Primitive? Ilka thought. Why, this ancient land had had a flowering civilization when the English were little more than aborigines. But she did not speak her thoughts.

"I suppose you're all set for the big push tomorrow," Leighton said.

"Yes. The fireworks start at dawn — if the devils don't surrender this evening. I think they may, you know."

It was a matter of complete indifference to the noble lord, Ilka thought, whether they did or not.

"Perhaps," Leighton said. He doubted very much that the nationalists, hopeless as their plight was, would surrender. Not after the news of the executions. But he had sworn to himself that he would not mention that subject this afternoon. "They would avoid a terrible slaughter if they did," he said.

"You can't say, Leighton, I'm not giving them every opportunity to spare themselves that."

"Perhaps, sir," Ilka broke in, "they're afraid you will string up their leaders — as you did this morning!"

She had not meant to say it. The words had suddenly spilled out. She saw Harold frown. Even Stanhope's imperturbable face flushed.

"My dear Mrs. Leighton, I am aware of how you feel — and how the consul-general feels — about my having let justice take its course. But I want you to know that all through yesterday and deep into the night I wrestled with my conscience. In the end my duty seemed clear. That was all there was to it."

If only she could come to such concise conclusions — and with a clear conscience, Ilka thought. Like this petrified old man. Like Singh . . .

"I do think," the governor was saying, "that the three of us have, if I may say so, just about exhausted that subject."

"I am sorry," Ilka said. She was hurt by Harold's obvious displeasure. It had been rash of her to blurt out her feelings like that; she should have been more careful. The old gentleman, though, was right. They had exhausted the subject. There was nothing more to *say*.

"By the way, Leighton," Lord Branhope said, recovering his composure and speaking expansively. "I think I shall have a plane tomorrow for your senator."

"That would be a great help," Leighton said.

[203]

"Any word about your courier plane?"

"No. It seems to be permanently grounded in Delhi."

A servant came in, bowed, and announced that the first guests were arriving. Ilka sprang up, followed by the other two.

"If you will excuse me, Lord Branhope," Ilka said.

"We are coming with you," Leighton said. He was not quite sure what protocol called for, except that it would never do to leave the governor-general alone in his living room.

"If I may have one short word with you, Leighton," Branhope said. He turned to Ilka. "Will you pardon me for detaining your husband one second?"

"That's perfectly all right, Your Excellency," Ilka smiled. But it wasn't. It worried her. The old man knew something he didn't want her to hear. Was he setting a trap? That would snare Singh? Was he tipping Harold off so that she might be spared?

"I shall join you in an instant, Ilka," Leighton said, as she hurried out through the veranda.

"About the senator, Leighton —"

"Has he been pestering you?"

"Well, he has been camping on my doorstep, so to speak. A strange sort of a fellow, isn't he? Quite a talker!"

"In Americanese, Governor," Branhope smiled, "we would call him a bit of a windbag."

"What I wanted you to know, Leighton," Branhope

said, "was that I had to straighten out the old boy about you."

"About me?"

"He had some outlandish idea that you weren't doing enough for him, that you lacked energy for your job, that you weren't aggressive enough, and all that rot."

"You put him straight, you say?"

"I told him, in the first place, that you practically ran this country, that you were at me every moment to do this, and not to do that. I told him that however much I resented your interference, you were just about the ablest diplomat I've ever known and that I hoped the U. S. Senate would have sense enough to recognize it and reward you."

"Despite the exaggeration, I appreciate that," Leighton said. The old man's affection for him, he thought, was quite touching. Well, Branhope had his points. He would miss working with him. Leighton got up.

"One more thing, Leighton, and I apologize for keeping you," Branhope said, taking him by the arm. "That Sikh lawyer fellow, Govind Singh. We can't find him. Uh . . . you don't have any idea yourself . . ."

"If I did, Governor," Leighton smiled, "I couldn't tell you."

"I remember your telling me once he was in love with your beautiful daughter, and I was just wondering . . ."

Again Leighton broke in: "I said, remember, *she* was

in love with *him!* But that's all over now. Singh's skipping away, for one thing, solved that."

"I was just wondering, Leighton, whether he hadn't sent her some word. People in love do that, you know. We've watched your mail . . ."

"That wasn't very nice of you, sir," Leighton said, smiling. They had strolled as far as the veranda now and Leighton was anxious to get to Ilka's side and start receiving the guests. It would not look quite proper to have Ilka greeting them alone.

"She hasn't heard from him?" Lord Branhope was asking.

"If I knew, Governor, I wouldn't say." Leighton took Branhope's arm and guided him down the steps to the garden.

"You're an admirable fellow, Leighton," the governor said, and Harold thought he knew how the old man meant it. Admiration and affection were all to the good, if you could inspire them. But respect came first, especially with a gentleman of the old school, of the past.

Singh kept pretty well out of the garden all afternoon. There was no telling how many Sikh and Hindu plainclothesmen the C.I.D. had planted among the guests. They were for the most part a shabby lot. A good many of them, he knew, were working for the Nationalist Supreme Council too. Whichever way the struggle went, they hoped to benefit. Singh had had dealings with a few of them. He did not want to risk being recognized. Being on the whole stupid louts, and lazy to boot, they would probably not come within a mile of seeing through his disguise. Besides, most of them would soon be tight on the Leightons' punch, champagne and whisky. But he would take no chances. As it was, he had had a narrow escape before the party had even started.

What a silly fool he had been to let himself be almost caught — and red-handed! Mrs. Leighton was right. He remembered her warning him that the best-laid plans went astray, that a lot of things you hadn't counted on could happen. He had been very arrogant with her. He had thought of everything, he had boasted. It was necessary of course to keep up her resolve. Could he count on it now? In the end? He was sure of it — or was he? She was a very strong woman, at heart. She had a vein of iron in her that he liked. And her whole life, like his, had led — had it not? — to this supreme moment when all the years of ceaseless talk culminated in one blinding instant of action. That was his understanding, anyway, arrived at soberly after more than a year of hearing her out and sizing her up. She agreed that what they were doing was right, was simple justice — a necessity.

But today, more than ever before in recent days, one single doubt kept rising to plague him. It was not about what had to be done — he would do it one way or another, within an hour or two now. But had it been right to involve her? This was not her country, after all;

not really her fight, as it was his. She had been right, though he had argued against her, in saying she had obligations quite other than his. To her husband, above all — and her child. And also to her adopted country. Still, it was too late to go into that now. She had involved herself inextricably by taking him in, knowing full well why he wanted to come here. Or was that true — absolutely? She had wanted to give him refuge, to save him from — well, old Branhope, if he had found him, probably would have thrown him to a court-martial and most certainly would have let the sentence stick. She had provided a hiding place. Was that all? No, she had gone ahead with him in his plans. She had, to be sure, had her moments of uncertainty. But if they had been serious she could have asked him to leave. He could now get away to the hills without much risk. But she had not suggested such a thing.

Still, he was skating around the core of what concerned him most. Wasn't it that he could not go through with this act if there was any possibility of her being caught? He honestly did not see how the authorities could get anything on her. He would never breathe a word of it no matter what they put him through — if they caught him, and he felt confident he could get away. The police would never stop the consul-general's official car, not for a few minutes anyway, and by that time he would be safely in the hills. In that case, who would ever suspect Mrs. Leighton?

But supposing he did get caught? It was always possible. If he were successful in getting the old man, he did not much care. He would owe his life to the Almighty, much more so than some of his friends who were getting killed in the fighting down by the docks. He was not worrying too much about that. And he knew he would be strong enough not even to utter Mrs. Leighton's name, regardless of the screws they put to him.

What frightened him was that she might tell on herself. She was so weak on that point . . . Or was it strength? Was it some sense of honor, of solidarity beyond his own? Was it — he did not like even to think the word — love? No. It couldn't be. She had made that fairly plain. Despite his own feelings, which he had tried to repress, they had kept love out. And yet, she must know that at heart he loved her much too deeply to want her to share his possible end. That must never happen! The governor's life was not worth hers . . .

Yet, probably there would be no more opportunity before the fatal moment to have a last word with her, to impress on her again that regardless of what happened she must keep her lips sealed about herself.

Perhaps, then, it would be best not even to take that risk, best to scrap their plan, and, instead, for him to saunter out to the garden alone, with the tray of drinks on his shoulder, watch for a favorable moment and do it alone, when she was not even around. An innocent person or two might get hurt, or even killed. But that would be preferable to involving her fatally. After all, she had given him this opportunity to do it here, now. That was enough.

Was it, though?

When he had gone out to the garden the first time to reconnoiter and to practice balancing the large tray on his shoulder without spilling the drinks, he had sensed that the governor was surrounded by native plainclothesmen posing as guests. The two uniformed English C.I.D. inspectors kept moving about at Branhope's heels, their eyes alert.

Only Mrs. Leighton, the hostess, the consul-general's wife, could lure the old man away from this protective guard. Alone, Singh might not be able to penetrate it, or, if he did, he might be struck down lightninglike in the very moment of acting, at the very second of pulling his gun from his coat pocket, before he could fire.

For the first time since the plan had sprouted in his mind, Singh found himself torn by insidious doubts: not what to do, but how.

The senator was having the time of his life. Leighton might not be any great shakes as a consul-general but he certainly knew how to throw a gracious party — or at least his beautiful wife knew how. The bourbon was absolutely the best he had ever stumbled into outside of Louisville, Kentucky. He had said as much to Lord Branhope and even persuaded the old boy to see for himself.

The senator was pleased that he had made such a strong impression on this old Roman in the few days he had been here. The governor-general had just taken him aside and promised him a British bomber tomorrow to fly him out to India. His worries were over. He would overlook that little discourtesy of the overzealous detectives ransacking his bags. He could relax now and enjoy himself — with all the pretty ladies in their charming summer frocks. And he could let himself go a little with the bourbon. Thank God, he could carry his likker! That was more than he could say of those two Yankee businessmen. The Irishman was really high and the oilman was becoming boisterous. It was rather embarrassing for a United States Senator to see his compatriots forgetting themselves on a national holiday before all these foreigners.

"They get lonely out here," Snow said. "Liquor helps, I suppose."

"They ought to be men enough to carry it better," the senator snorted. "Now take our gracious hostess," he went on, to Snow's surprise. "I believe I have observed her putting down quite a few. But you would never know it. She looks and acts like a queen."

"I doubt if she has had half as many as you and I, Senator," Snow said, as blandly as he could. "I have known Ilka Leighton since before she was married. She is really very temperate, Senator."

"I'm not blaming her, Snow. I'm admiring her — the way she carries it."

"She's frightfully tired, poor thing," Snow said quickly. "She has been under quite a strain, you know, the last few weeks. And it was quite a job, I imagine, organizing this affair. She did it all herself, you know."

"A remarkable woman. And extremely attractive, isn't she," the senator said, casting his eyes about the garden for a glimpse of her. "But strange too," he added.

"Interesting rather than strange, I would say," Snow answered.

"I think I detected a trace of an accent in her speech."

"Did you?"

"What is she, anyway?" Senator Bridgehorn asked.

"Originally Hungarian."

"Foreign, anyway. Well that solves it," the senator said, apparently relieved. "You know, Snow, I was instrumental in getting a law passed against our diplomats marrying foreign women."

"It was a stupid law, Senator — if you'll pardon me."

"They're not good for American diplomats — I mean, generally speaking."

"This one, sir, has been very good for this particular diplomat," Snow said with some emphasis.

He was a little worried about Ilka. He did not know how Leighton had resolved his uneasiness about her. Harold had ceased confiding in him after first bringing the matter up. Probably, as he, Snow, had believed all along, there had been nothing to it. What concerned him was that Ilka, after five years of it out here, was very run down. The disturbances of the past few weeks had keyed her up, as they had all of them, though her most of all. But because she lacked the normal means of release which most people like himself had when the tensions within built up, she might be, he had begun to fear, near the point of cracking up. If only she had a safety valve, as almost everyone had, to release the pressure from within when it became too high.

More than once recently he had taken her aside, walked her out to the garden, and tried to draw her out. If, as an old friend, he could get her to talk herself out in complete confidence, that would help to relieve the pressure. But he had been unsuccessful. She seemed more guarded than ever before, as if she did not quite trust even him. And though she was obviously aching from fatigue, she remained, he could feel, more wrought up than the circumstances, bad as they were, seemed to him to justify.

Ilka had, he noticed, been drinking a little more than usual. Perhaps in this one instance even a little excessive drinking would help; it might provide a release. As for this afternoon, the senator had not been wholly wrong. Snow had seen her snatching — almost desperately, he thought — more than one whisky and soda off the passing trays. It showed in the deep color in her cheeks, in the slight blear in her beautiful black eyes that were usually so sparkling and clear. Perhaps only he, who knew her so well, noticed. Harold was much too busy to see, he was sure. And perhaps, too, imbibing a few strong drinks was the only way to cope with the ordeal of seeing the garden party, on which she had worked so strenuously, through in the scorching heat of the sunburnt afternoon.

All this ghastly afternoon Ilka Leighton felt herself moving around mechanically in a daze. Despite the deadly heat she was conscious of not perspiring; in fact she felt constant chills. She propelled herself about automatically, greeting guests, conversing with them here and there, fiercely forcing a smile, desperately striving to keep her voice and manner as natural as possible and wondering what it was she was saying. Several times she thought she could not go on. Once, midway through the afternoon, fearing that she would faint, she looked frantically around for Bob Snow. She would get him to take her away for a short drive in the consulate car — that would solve everything, more than good old Bob could possibly imagine. She could explain to Harold that she felt momentarily ill and ask him to carry on for a few minutes. Bob would whisk her four or five miles further up in the hills. The cooler air would revive her. It would . . . But Bob Snow and the senator were engaged in some sort of discussion with Lord Branhope. She could not get his attention. A waiter passed. She snatched another drink. She must watch that. She had already taken more than was wise. But how else go on?

She had not seen Singh all afternoon. Perhaps he was flitting about the lawn, but she had not recognized him. From a little distance all the Sikh servants, in their long beards, turbans and fancy livery, looked the same. Each time one came by with a tray of champagne, she eyed him closely. But not once was it Singh. Perhaps he thought it too dangerous to come out. Perhaps, in the haze she was in, she wouldn't have made him out if he did.

She kept glancing at her wrist watch. Four-forty-five. Five o'clock. Five-twenty. Five-thirty. At five-thirty, she slipped away to the house. She felt giddy. She would sit down for a moment in the living room, drink another highball, smoke a cigarette and this time get hold of herself. Singh might come in for what he thought would be a last word before . . . Well, it would be the last word. She would be stern. She would tell him it was off. She was sorry; but she would not go through with it. She would not let him argue. There would be no time for that, anyway. She would simply tell him, and turn away without a further word, as he had turned away from her an hour or so ago in this very room. And then she would make her way to the garden and stand at Harold's side to bid the departing guests farewell, beginning with the noble lord. Ah, if the smiling, arrogant, cruel old man could only know her thoughts as she said good-by:

that she had saved him from certain death, that he owed his life, such as it was, to her. Against her better judgment, she had decided to spare him, old tyrant and murderer that he was. But instead, of course, she would say something banal, utter one last ringing diplomatic cliché, and that would be that. He would be gone. Safely . . .

A figure came hurrying through from the veranda with an empty tray in his arm. Ilka sprang up. It must be . . .

"Singh!" she cried.

"It's time!" Singh said.

"Singh! I . . ."

"The old man's had about enough. I shall fetch a fresh tray. You fetch him!"

Before she could utter a further sound, Singh darted through the door toward the kitchen.

From that second on, as far as she could recall later, she had sunk back into a trance. Strange things happened. She remembered that as she was going down the steps to the garden, Isobel, darling, innocent Isobel, had come up.

"Mother! Are you feeling all right?" Isobel had asked, her open young face full of concern.

"I had a bit of a dizzy spell, darling — but I'm all right now. How lovely you look, my dear."

"Have you heard the big rumor?" Isobel had exclaimed, taking her arm as they walked down the garden. "... That they've arrested Singh! Everyone's talking about it!"

"Really?" Ilka had managed to say.

"Do you think it's true, Mother?"

"I wish it were!" She had mumbled it to herself, but Isobel had evidently heard.

"How horrible of you, Mother!" Isobel had cried.

"Not horrible ... No ..."

"But, Mother!"

And then, Ilka recalled, Harold had come up and, unknowingly, had sealed her fate.

"I was looking for you, darling," he said.

"I felt a little faint. I hope no one noticed my absence."

"Are you sure you're quite all right now, my dear?"

"Perfectly ... Are they starting to leave already?" She looked down on the vast throng.

"The governor is about ready to go." Harold spoke with relief. "He insists on having a last word with you. Just this once, Ilka, I would be grateful if you humored the old boy. Will you, my dear — for my sake, please?"

"Why certainly, Harold," she had said.

The old man, then, was playing inexorably into their hands, she was horrified to see. That must be the way God wanted it. She would never — would she? — have had the courage to take that next to the last step. Since Singh would not even listen to her, had she not intended simply to return to the garden, rejoin Harold and stand at his side and speak with him their farewells — leaving Singh waiting behind the door with his tray of champagne until the governor had gone and the wine in the little glasses on the tray had turned warm and stale?

She was sure of it, but now Lord Branhope was coming up to her. "My dear Mrs. Leighton, this has been a most charming occasion. Except for one thing. I have scarcely had a chance to exchange a word with you all afternoon."

Now it was, Ilka explained to herself afterward, that she felt caught up and swept helplessly on a current whose power and direction and final destination had been determined the day she was conceived. There was nothing she could do but float on with it to the end.

"I regret it as much as you do, Your Excellency," she had replied.

"Can't we get away for a moment from this mob?" he had suggested, lowering his voice, and as if moving in a dream she had led him up to the veranda and into the living room.

"This is a relief!" he had exclaimed, sinking onto the divan and mopping his great brow. "How I've stood this infernal climate all these years is beyond me."

"The summers are almost as bad at home — especially in Washington," she said.

"I can't believe it. Well, my dear Mrs. Leighton, whether they are or not, you will soon be there. And

I shall miss you more than I can say. I know I'm becoming a repetitious old man. But I did want to say it once more, to you alone."

"You are very gallant, Lord Branhope," Ilka said, and she was conscious of flashing a smile and of making her eyes light up.

"As I have told you a hundred times, you are, madame, the most beautiful, the most charming and easily the most interesting woman we have ever had in our little foreign colony here. You are, in truth, irreplaceable!"

"You . . . flatter me, Lord Branhope."

"Not that I have always understood you, Mrs. Leighton," Branhope smiled.

"Nor I perhaps you . . ." Ilka matched his smile.

"Well, that sort of thing has its attractions, don't you think?" Lord Branhope said.

"It does indeed," Ilka said. "But I am happy to think that in the end, despite our differences, we did achieve some kind of understanding of each other."

What was she saying? Harold had said to humor him. Singh had urged it . . . "Talk earnestly to him about your misunderstanding. Say you now see better his many problems . . . Praise him! Say how much Lady Branhope has meant to you! . . ." Those were Singh's very words. She looked over to the door to the dining room. It was shut. Was Singh standing behind it? And what — the thought suddenly brought beads of perspiration on her forehead — was the signal, if the door did open a crack? She could not remember. She would not try to remember.

"We are terribly sorry," Ilka heard herself saying, "that Lady Branhope could not be here for our little farewell."

"Not half so sorry as she must be, I assure you," the governor replied genially. "But you will be seeing her in England. Believe me, she will be looking forward to that!"

"Not half so much as we!" Ilka lied. They would soon be exhausting their subjects of polite conversation. In a moment the governor would take his leave. Why did the door not bulge open? She must cease staring at it. Had Branhope noticed?

"Poor dear, I'm afraid Lady Branhope is wearing herself out fixing the old place up," Ilka heard the governor say. "It got terribly run down, you know."

She saw the door move, or was she imagining it? A half inch. An inch. There was no mistaking it now. She looked at Branhope. He was smiling contentedly, no doubt, Ilka thought, at the recollection of his wife puttering about the ancient, rickety ancestral place. What was the signal? What had Singh said? . . . Lord Branhope moved as if to get up.

"One more thing, Lord Branhope!" she said desperately. She must clear up her soggy mind. She must think of the sign. Why had she been born with such a wretched memory? Singh must be standing there half out of his mind, cursing her. It must look to him like a betrayal. She turned to Branhope, looking searchingly into his eyes. Now was the moment she must see in him a cold-blooded murderer, a *henker*, a hangman. The sight of him must fill her with hate. But he was smiling affectionately and saying in his soft voice: "What is that, my dear Mrs. Leighton?"

For an instant she wanted to shout to him to get out. She would stand between him and the door. She would shield him as he moved safely out. He had asked her a question. What had prompted it?

"My dear friend," she said, clutching his hands. She would say how much she appreciated what he had done for her husband. That, at least, would be the truth. "I want you to know . . ."

She felt the door opening. Singh had not waited for any sign. Singh started to cross the room toward the veranda. He was balancing — precariously, she saw — a full tray of glasses of champagne. She could see the wine sparkling in them. Singh moved slowly, almost silently, toward the veranda. She should call out. In three, four, five seconds it would be too late. She saw Singh pause, and glance out toward the garden. He did not look back. She tried to give sound to her voice. Her throat was parched; her vocal cords did not respond. Singh took a step forward, and then another.

"Boy!" Ilka heard the governor cry out. "Just a minute!" She sank back in terror.

"Madame," Lord Branhope was beaming. "I would like to propose a farewell toast — with champagne." He turned to Singh. "Boy! Bring them over here, please!"

Singh turned. "Yes, sah'b." His bearded face was a blank, as Ilka saw it. She sat glued to the divan. Any movement at all had become impossible. She remembered what she was supposed to do. She tried to rise. Her limbs seemed to be paralyzed. She could not even look up. She must spring out of this stupor. She must this instant jump up, as Singh had said.

And then she felt Lord Branhope rising. "This is a happy coincidence," he was saying amiably . . . "Champagne for a farewell toast!"

Ilka forced herself to look up. The governor was reaching toward the tray, which Singh now held forward with outstretched hands. She watched him take two glasses and hold them up against the light from the window, as if admiring their golden, sparkling hue. Then he turned toward Ilka.

First, so far as she could recall later, there was a frightening crash. Singh let the tray drop. She saw him striving to balance it on the palm of one hand while he whipped into his side pocket with the other. She saw the tray tilt and slide off Singh's fingers to the floor, but the clatter of the shattering glass lasted only an instant. Singh was firing point-blank. Branhope, Ilka believed later, never had more than a second of shock. He had turned toward her, the two bubbling glasses in his hands. Before he could look back, they were spilling over her and he was slumping to the floor at her feet.

Chapter 15

THE NEWS of the cold-blooded assassination of the eminent Governor-General of Pawancore overshadowed in the world press the accounts of the government offensive that began at dawn the next day against the entrenched nationalists in the dock area of the capital. To an old journalist like Robert Agate Snow that was natural enough. He saw that to a world grown callous from the big wars, the big bombings, the atomic monster, the millions slain and maimed, the fighting here was only an unimportant skirmish. A few hundred souls, both brown and white, but mostly brown, were being slaughtered in as savage fighting as he had ever seen; but he was not surprised that the world outside seemed interested only in the violent death of one old man. People all over the globe were always fascinated by what they called murder: the killing of a lone individual. But if you multiplied that by a hundred or two a day, the public lost interest.

Snow was sitting on the veranda with Harold Leighton going over the first cables from Washington, which young Willoughby had brought over from the office. Because the unfortunate event had occurred in the home of an American consul-general and in the very presence of his wife, Snow knew it would be a front-page sensation at home. And from the dispatches he was reading, it was painfully evident that it was.

Some time before midnight last night both the *New York Times* and the Associated Press had cabled urgently to Snow, as the only American journalist they knew to be on the spot, asking him to file a full story. He had declined. He was not going to make the plight of the stricken Leightons any worse than it was. He must do what he could to try to shield Ilka.

He was not sure how much the authorities suspected her. For him, as certainly for Leighton, though Harold had not yet steeled himself to mention it, the news of the apprehension and arrest of Singh could lead to only one conclusion.

Within a few minutes of the shooting Singh had been caught. The consul-general's official car, in which he had tried to get away, had been stopped at a government roadblock on the outskirts of the capital. An English C.I.D. officer, who had not yet heard of the crime, became suspicious that the sole passenger in the American consular car was a native. He questioned him, he started to search him, and when the Sikh resisted there was a scuffle in which the man's false beard and wig were yanked off and a still-warm revolver, its barrel empty, was uncovered. The officer had recognized Singh at once, and since he knew him to be one of the few nationalist leaders still at large, had arrested him on the spot. He had then telephoned his superiors to report. It was only then that he realized, to his amazement, what a catch he had made. All this Snow learned when he called early in the evening at C.I.D. headquarters.

And then at midnight had come a special bulletin from Government House. It confirmed that Govind Singh had been arrested and said that he had made a full confession of the assassination. It was signed by General Sir Norman Cunningham, Commander-in-Chief, British Forces, and Acting Governor-General. Leighton, accompanied by Senator Bridgehorn, had immediately driven to Government House to offer the acting governor the official condolences of the United States government as well as their own. And Leighton had put himself at the disposal of the general in helping to get to the bottom of the crime.

Cunningham had been borrowed by Lord Branhope from the Indian Army but a month before to take charge of putting down the rebellion, and Leighton scarcely knew him. He was a bluff soldier who seemed to Leighton to be typical of the general officers he had met in the Indian Army. He did not appear to be very upset by what had happened; or perhaps, Leighton thought, it was merely that a man of his lifelong training didn't show it. He was courteous to his two visitors. He

[226]

thanked them for their call. He hoped Mrs. Leighton was recovering from the shock. And he assured them that his full-scale attack on the insurgents would go through as scheduled at dawn.

As for the culprit, he himself had questioned him and had had no difficulty in drawing out a full confession. The evidence had overwhelmed the poor man. He had been caught red-handed trying to escape from the scene of the crime in the consul-general's car. The revolver found on him, an old German Mauser, was obviously the one which had fired the fatal shots. They had established that from a bullet found embedded in the leg of a divan. And the man's fingerprints matched those found on some tray on the floor of the living room. Mrs. Leighton, the only witness to the actual event, already had told them that it was one of the waiters who had fired. It was obvious that the demented young lawyer had disguised himself as a servant — just how, without the knowledge of the Leightons or of the C.I.D., they would have to look into; there were certainly accomplices in addition to the consular chauffeur.

The young fanatic had insisted there were none, that he had planned and executed the deed alone and had forced the Leighton chauffeur at gun point to drive him away. That was obviously rubbish. The general had no doubt they could eventually persuade the young man to talk further. In the meantime he had ordered the C.I.D. to press the investigation. Mrs. Leighton, he knew —

as soon as she recovered from the shock — would be of great help. He understood she had been a little incoherent in her first account, which was only natural.

"Believe me, sir," he concluded, addressing Leighton, "we regret this embarrassment to you and your family."

"We shall do everything possible, General," Leighton responded, "to aid you in this investigation."

"And if I can be of any help, sir, please call on me," the senator added. Leighton was thankful that Bridgehorn had let him do most of the talking. The senator, too, like Ilka, seemed still to be in a state of shock. But when he opened up, it might not be helpful.

Leighton was not really concerned with what a powerful and dyspeptic United States Senator might do about an American consul who had been so careless of security as to allow a governor-general to be assassinated in his home. His career was probably ruined, but he did not even care about that. For the last hour or two he had been consumed with one burning thought: to get Ilka out of this.

Ilka, frozen with shock, had watched Singh, his gun still smoking, stoop down to look at the crumpled, bleeding body, as if to make sure there was no more life in it. He had looked up, given her one unforgettable glance of triumph, and then had scrambled away.

His going seemed to release her. Instinctively she knelt over Branhope, overcoming an instant of horror at the sight of the blood oozing out of the back of his neck, to unloosen his tie and collar. She reached for his wrist to feel his pulse and then bedlam broke loose. The first to rush into the room were the two inspectors, followed by Harold and Bob Snow. They were all, she remembered later, breathing heavily. They must have come running a long way. Before she could get her thumb on the wrist to take the pulse, the room was jammed with shouting, gesticulating figures, native and white, guests and servants, all pressing around her.

"Stand back! Stand back!" she heard one of the inspectors shout. The other was kneeling beside her over Branhope. He thrust away her hand which still gripped the governor's wrist and himself began to take the pulse. The room suddenly became still. She thought she could detect Harold breathing heavily just behind her. She gazed at the inspector's hardened, sunburnt face. Perhaps . . . Perhaps! . . . The man was turning to her and she knew from his eyes before he spoke.

"It's all over," the inspector said quietly.

"Oh, my God!"

She felt the room caving in on her. Harold was stooping to catch her in his arms as she sank back. He was mumbling something and then all was dark.

When she regained consciousness she found herself lying on the divan. Harold, the first inspector and Snow were sitting opposite her; except for them the room seemed empty. She looked hastily down at her side, where Branhope had fallen. He was not there. She looked at the three men.

"What . . . happened?"

"That's what we want you to tell us, madame," the inspector said.

"How long have I . . . been . . ."

"Only a few minutes, darling," Harold said, bending forward to take her hand. "Are you all right now?" He patted her hand. Slowly she sat up and took in her husband's face. It bore a terrible desolation. And yet he was trying to smile, consolingly. He turned to the officer: "I think she can tell us now . . . Ilka," he said to her softly, "what happened?"

She stared at him, trying to move her lips.

"You saw it, madame," the inspector said.

"Yes . . ."

"Tell us, please . . . how it happened."

She stared again at him. "He . . . he . . . shot him."

"Who shot him?"

"A . . . a man . . ."

"Native?"

Ilka was becoming gradually more alert; she felt the officer closing in on her. She must try . . .

"Yes," she said.

"Hindu? Sikh?" the inspector pressed her.

"He had a beard . . ." By now Singh would have shed his. And in the car he would have got rid of his servant's togs. By now he must be safely away. She felt quite awake. How much should she tell this man? She had to say something . . .

"A Sikh, then — is that right?"

"One of the servants," Ilka said.

"Yes, we judged so from the evidence here," the inspector said, pointing to the floor. Ilka looked down. The overturned tray lay there atop a heap of broken glass.

"Now, which servant was it?" the inspector asked.

"I . . . don't know."

"You don't know?"

"I . . . didn't recognize him."

"But certainly, Mrs. Leighton, you know your servants."

Ilka felt a panic coming over her. Why had she and Singh never discussed what she was to say?

"He was not one I recognized. He . . ." she started to say, but the inspector cut her short.

"It could have been someone disguised as a servant?"

"Yes," she said, relieved. "It must have been."

"You told me just before the party, I believe, that you had hired no extra servants for the occasion."

"That is true," Ilka answered.

"I can confirm that, Inspector," Harold put in quickly.

"Then how did this man slip in? How was he able to pass as a servant, I would like to know."

"I don't know, sir," Ilka replied.

Snow, who had been following the questioning with

mounting uneasiness, sensed Ilka's desperateness. "Inspector," he broke in, "perhaps you can find that out from the servants."

"I'm having them questioned now, sir," the inspector said. Snow saw Ilka wince.

"Now, Mrs. Leighton," the officer said. "Let's go back to the beginning. Please tell me, as fully as you can, just what happened. How did His Excellency happen to be in this room, in the first place?"

"He . . ." Ilka began, but this time Harold broke in.

"Inspector, I think I can tell you best about that, since it was my doing, so to speak . . ." Ilka was obviously in no condition to talk coherently; he would have to take over the answering, so far as he could. He did not like the turn the questioning was taking.

"Very well," the officer responded.

"Lord Branhope mentioned to me that he would like to have a word with Mrs. Leighton before he left," Leighton explained. "Obviously, to get away from the milling guests on the lawn, they had come up to the villa."

"Just a minute," the officer interrupted. "Mrs. Leighton, who suggested coming up to the villa?"

"Lord Branhope!" Ilka could say it with some emphasis. That, at least, was the truth.

"Very well. You came up here — to this living room. Now go on from there, please," the inspector said.

"I can't . . . I can't! . . ." Ilka began to sob. ". . . It was too terrible! . . . No! . . ."

"I appreciate your feelings, Mrs. Leighton," the officer said kindly. "But you understand that you are the only one who can help us, and I'm sure you wish to . . ."

"Yes! . . . Yes! . . . I do! . . . But it was too ghastly! . . . Too . . . *No!* . . . I can't . . . I . . ." She was weeping hysterically now, and both Snow and Leighton saw they must quickly intervene

"Please, Mrs. Leighton!" the inspector begged.

"Officer!" Harold spoke up.

". . . I told you . . . He shot . . . He kept firing . . . He . . ." Ilka mumbled between sobs.

"Inspector," Harold said firmly above the crescendo of Ilka's sobbing, "it is obvious that my wife is in no condition to go on. You can understand that it has been a terrible shock to her."

"Certainly, sir," the officer readily assented.

"I would suggest that we continue this tomorrow morning, after she has had a chance to rest and to recover."

"Very well, sir," the inspector said. "Tomorrow morning, then. In the meantime, sir, I am having in some special officers to go over the tray there for fingerprints and to see if there are any stray bullets about."

"Let us hope, Inspector," Leighton said, "they will turn up some clues."

He had helped his prostrate wife up to the bedroom, given her a strong sedative and sat by her bedside as she slowly subsided into sleep. Not until Snow came back from C.I.D. headquarters that evening with the fateful news of Singh's arrest did he begin to realize what must have happened and what he faced.

Chapter 16

ONE DAY shortly before noon, Isobel Leighton returned to the villa to find her mother at her desk in the living room, absorbed in writing. Isobel had gone off just after dawn with her father, Bob Snow and the senator to watch the final assault on a last remnant of the insurgents who still held out in the debris of some shattered warehouses by the water's edge.

Ilka, scribbling away at her desk, had noticed how strangely still the morning had suddenly become. The battle must be over. It had thundered all through this nightmare of a week. Night and day the planes had roared over their rooftop and the explosion of the bombs and of the shells from the gunboats and the government artillery and tanks had rocked the city and cast over it a thick pall of smoke that even the tropical sun could not penetrate, leaving one choking in the stifling haze and accentuating her own feeling of approaching doom.

In the turmoil of the city only a brief funeral service for Lord Branhope had been possible. Lady Branhope had flown out from London in a military transport plane and after the abbreviated ceremony at Government House, which itself resembled an entrenched camp, had flown back to England with the body. Ilka had wept through most of the funeral service. It was pitiful to see the widow so stricken; she who had always seemed to Ilka to be a cold, bloodless creature without human emotions except when it came to horses and dogs and flowers. Ilka had wanted to pour out her own shattered feelings to the lady; she had asked to see her alone. But Harold would not have it, and when they both saw her for a few moments after the funeral, Lady Branhope was tense but cool, as if, Ilka thought, she were holding back from uttering a terrible curse on them for allowing her husband to be callously murdered in their home.

The senator was still here. Once the government offensive had begun, it had proved impossible to procure transportation for him. General Cunningham had informed Harold he could not possibly spare one of his bombers until the rebels had been wiped out. Delhi had wired that it was holding the courier plane until the fighting died down. Senator Bridgehorn had become even more irascible than before; Snow had told them that the man went about muttering: "This is a hell of a family to represent the U.S.A.!" And Harold had told her of a cable Bridgehorn had sent by consular code to the Department urging Leighton's replacement immediately. Little did the senator know that *that* was exactly what they both wanted!

Or was it? Harold certainly. But she? Ilka could not make up her mind. She was aware of Leighton's growing anxiety about her — and of Bob Snow's. All week long Harold had insisted on taking part in every interrogation. Whenever she weakened, whenever she appeared to be trapped, Harold had plunged in to rescue her. But did she, now, want to be rescued? For her husband's sake, yes. For her own? Coward that she was, she did not think so. She had to balance what she owed Harold, the obligation not to destroy him, against consideration of the other thing.

The news of Singh's quick capture had stunned her. She had been sure he would get away. So many unbelievable things had happened that they had not foreseen: the roadblock, the white officer's suspicions, his searching of Singh, Singh's resistance, the disguise falling away, the still-warm pistol found; and then, to make the guilt inescapable, the fingerprints on the tray, the stray bullet that got lodged in a leg of the divan.

Probably, though, from the way he had talked to her those last ghastly hours, Singh would have confessed anyway, once he was caught. Had he not made it plain to her that if he were successful, he did not much care what happened to him? Incredibly! he had been much more concerned about her. She must never breathe a word about her own part. He had made that a condition for going ahead.

She knew he had not implicated her. General Cunningham had told Harold of Singh's insistence that there were no accomplices. But it made her gasp to think what they were doing to make him talk! Out here in Asia they had a hundred refinements of torture that slowly ground the will out of a prisoner. The police, the C.I.D., must already have begun with them!

Was there any justification at all for her to allow that to go on? She had the power to halt it. She had only to speak up. Not to do so — was that not the height of cowardice, of dishonor, not to mention inhumanity? That was what she had to balance against her obligations not to wreck Harold Leighton's life. For, to be coldly factual about it, she knew that to expose herself as an accomplice in the murder, to take the consequences and go to prison — or perhaps, like Singh, to the gallows, for they would surely hang him as soon as they thought they had squeezed the last bit of information out of him — would doom her husband to a life worse than death. Would that not be even a more horrible crime than the one she had just committed, and, in this instance, done to a decent, kindly, upright man whom she loved, respected, and to whom she felt joined everlastingly?

But there was something else. A man had been slain, and she was partly responsible for it. Was it right to try to escape punishment? Even when Singh had insisted that she must? For herself, she was quite ready to accept it, as Singh had done for himself.

And now, today, she must make her decision. She and

Harold had agreed to meet the C.I.D. immediately after lunch for one last interrogation. She knew, from the hammering of the questions all week, what they would persist in asking. How did Govind Singh get into the Leighton household disguised as a servant? Since the other servants had divulged that he had worked there for several days prior to the garden party, how was it possible for Mr. and Mrs. Leighton and their daughter not to have recognized him? He had frequented their home for years. They knew him well. Granted that his disguise may have concealed his looks, did they not recognize his voice? Mrs. Leighton, the servants had testified, had been seen conversing with him in the garden on more than one occasion up to the very eve of the fatal day. Had her suspicions not been aroused?

What use was it to evade them any longer? They had her. Harold must see that. He had not tried once to question her privately about anything. But it was obvious to her that he knew, being ignorant only of the details.

As soon as the others had left that early morning to see the final engagement down by the docks, Ilka had sat down at her desk and started to write.

She put down her pen as Isobel came in.

"Do I disturb you, Mother?" Isabel asked.

"No." Ilka looked down at the half-filled page on top of the sheaf of papers. She had almost finished.

"It's all over, Mother."

"What?" She was thinking that she must have filled at least twenty sheets. It had all come out so easily . . .

"The fighting. They wiped out the last gallant little band."

"Wiped them out?" Ilka looked up.

"It was frightful to see. They refused to surrender. The place is a shambles. The stench — I couldn't stand it."

"Of the dead?"

"Yes. There must have been hundreds. Some of them buried in the debris all week."

"Hundreds? What Singh stirred up!"

"Mother!" Isobel cried. "What will they do to him!"

Now that she had almost finished writing, Ilka felt strangely relaxed — almost serene. "What do you suppose?" she said quietly.

"I don't know! I can't bear to think of it!" Ilka saw Isobel's eyes watering. She was a high-strung child, despite her innocence.

"Perhaps the acting governor will save him," Ilka said.

"Set him free!"

"No — but not hang him. Give him instead — life on the malaria islands, which is perhaps worse."

"Mother, they can't! I'm sure he's innocent!"

"He killed the governor . . . Right over there," Ilka said, pointing to the divan. She was surprised that she could speak of it so calmly. But everything had now become so clear.

"How can you say that, Mother! You've told us a dozen times you didn't know who it was — you couldn't recognize him!"

"Singh confessed."

"Perhaps they tortured him! You say anything they want if they torture you!" Isobel was shuddering at the thought, Ilka saw.

"Perhaps," she said, feeling a smile break out on her face that shocked the younger one, "he was proud to confess." Ilka turned back to her writing and grasped her pen. ". . . And that's what I . . ." She stopped herself.

"What!"

"Never mind . . ."

Ilka got up and put her hands on her daughter's shoulders. "Darling, you must try to forget. Soon you will be ten thousand miles away from here." She looked into the guileless but tormented eyes. ". . . You loved him, didn't you?"

Isobel was sobbing. "Yes," she said.

"I can understand," Ilka said. She held her daughter closely for a moment, and then released her. "Back home, you can make a new start. In college there, you will be in a new world."

"I don't want to go home. I don't want to go to college," Isobel answered.

"I know. But in time, darling, you will see things differently. You know the old saying: Time is a great healer." Ilka again took her daughter's hands. "You are so young . . . and beautiful . . ."

Isobel gently broke away. "Not half so beautiful as you, Mother," she said, and Ilka was pained at the look of adoration in the youthful eyes. Isobel took a step or two toward the veranda, peered out at the garden and then turned back.

"Mother," Isobel said. "Did you have the faintest idea that Singh . . . that he could do it?"

It was Ilka's turn to be taken back. It was not to this innocent young creature that she was ready to talk.

"No," Ilka said.

"Did Singh ever give you the faintest hint?"

"No." Ilka looked at Isobel sharply.

"Somehow . . ." Isobel said, and halted.

"Yes? . . ."

". . . In some way . . . I felt he was closer to you than to me."

"Don't talk nonsense," Ilka said. Had this immature child been more discerning than she had imagined?

"Somehow . . . I felt it . . . these last months, at least," Isobel said.

"I admired Singh . . . For his ideals . . . his courage . . ."

"Yes!"

Isobel's pathetic earnestness was touching a fatal chord. "Deep down," Ilka murmured, "there was in him a flame. It burned very pure . . ." Ilka caught herself up. "What am I saying! . . ."

"What I think too, Mother!"

Ilka stood up. "You must run along now, dear. I have some rather urgent letters to finish."

"I'm sorry, Mother. I didn't mean to interrupt you."

"I'm glad you did . . . Darling, how about some tennis this afternoon?"

"Everett has to work — on some report."

"Everett Willoughby? I rather like that young man, Isobel."

"I'm beginning to, too," Isobel smiled.

"Perhaps you can get the senator to play some golf, then. Take him out of Harold's hair for a moment."

"It would probably give him a heart attack — in this heat, and after what he saw this morning."

"All the better!" Ilka said, and they both laughed.

"Good-by, Mother!"

Ilka sat down at her desk, staring at the half-finished page. "Lies . . . lies . . . to my own daughter . . ." she mumbled to herself. "But this . . ." she took up the sheaf of papers . . . "this is the truth!"

She was reading over what she had written when she heard Harold's car come up the driveway. As he entered the living room, she was struck by how haggard he looked.

"Am I intruding?" he said softly, coming over to kiss her on the forehead.

"No, darling. But I didn't expect you for lunch." She would have liked an hour more, she thought, to ponder what she had written.

"Bob Snow and the senator went off to lunch at Government House with Cunningham," Leighton said. "I begged off. I didn't feel up to joining in any victory celebration."

"Isobel was just here. She said it was all over."

"Yes. It is . . . What a bloody mess! This morning it was a massacre."

"Was it necessary?"

"Well, the devils wouldn't surrender. What Singh did obviously steamed them up all week. I myself went out to them this morning during a momentary truce and begged them to give up. But they wouldn't listen. They fought to the last man. It was tough to have to look at."

"I suppose," Ilka said, "it will teach the rest a lesson."

"Yes, that the government means business, as poor old Branhope would have said."

"Everyone safe at the consulate?" Ilka asked.

"Yes, including the senator. Well, at last we'll be getting *him* out of here." Leighton put his hands on her shoulders. "Darling, I have news for you! I had a cable from the Department. They've given the job to Campbell — remember, he was with us in Shanghai. We can leave next week. How do you like that, darling?"

"I can't believe it, Harold," Ilka said, trying her best to brighten up, at least for the moment.

"I told Bob," Leighton said. "He still insists we go back by way of Europe and take a month off with him in the Tyrol. You remember that place near Innsbruck where we used to ski? And where we went after our wedding? He wants to go there. How does that suit you?"

"Fine," Ilka said, "though it is much too early to ski." The very thought of getting away to that beautiful land of happy, youthful memories had lifted Harold to the skies. The haggard look in his face, she saw, had disappeared. A month in the Tyrol was a dream of utter loveliness to her as well, but now, this afternoon, it would be shattered for both of them.

"We can climb mountains, my dear, and we can cool off — after five years of being boiled and roasted here."

"It sounds too beautiful to be true," Ilka said.

"I think we both have it coming," Leighton said, and Ilka suddenly felt him peering over her shoulder at the pile of scribbled sheets that lay before her on the desk.

"You were writing?" Harold asked. His tone was so kindly, so innocent, so trusting that she felt as if her heart were being pierced. But now she would have to steel herself; she would have to be implacable.

"Yes," she said.

"May I be inquisitive, darling, and ask what?"

Ilka looked up and stared at him. This final act would be more wrenching than even the one with Singh.

"Something . . . for the . . . police!" she blurted out.

"The police!"

"A sort of . . . confession!"

"I don't understand, Ilka." And then she saw his eyes suddenly strain at the sockets. "You mean . . . !"

She must go through with this calmly, coldly.

"Yes," she said. "You know what I mean."

"And you intend to give it to the police!"

In all their long years she had never seen in him a look of such desperation. If only there had been some possible way of avoiding this . . .

"Who else?" she said.

"Ilka, you can't!"

"I must!"

"I won't let you!"

He was shouting it, the words he had never used in all their life, and each cry of despair was piercing her and tearing her apart. Yet she felt that all that she was, or had wanted to be, was driving her on inexorably though she be torn in a hundred pieces.

"They're coming in a few minutes, you know," she said, glancing at her watch.

"Who?"

"The police. The C.I.D."

"So they are — I remember now," Harold said, lower-

[246]

ing his voice. "Well, we've told them all we know — a dozen times over."

"Not all *I* know," Ilka said, looking him squarely in the face.

"What!"

"What I did!"

As if the better to gain control of himself, Leighton drew back from her and started to pace the floor. Then he stopped.

"My dear Ilka, don't you see! Even if what you are hinting at is true — and I am far from believing it — it isn't going to help anyone to come out with it."

"It may do Singh some good," Ilka said. "Subtract from his guilt. My share."

Harold was calmer now, she was glad to see. They could reason out quietly what had to be done.

"There is no chance for Singh," Leighton said. "You know that. He will hang."

Ilka winced. "Yes," she said, after a moment. "I suppose he will."

"There is nothing, really, you can do . . . to save him."

She did not answer. It was true. But what Harold did not see was that there was something she could do to save herself, though not in the way he was thinking. He was pacing the floor again.

"You know, Ilka, what I cannot understand? . . . He had some strange hold on you . . ."

"Perhaps . . . And perhaps I on him . . ."

"What!"

"One never really understands a human relationship. It is always a mystery. Even ours . . ."

"Yes . . . But ours has been good . . . and durable."

". . . And beautiful," Ilka whispered.

He took her by the arm and led her to the divan. "Singh," Harold said, "belonged to another world. Even you could never get to know him."

"Are you so sure?" Ilka said. "There are universal things, Harold, that affect us all . . . from whatever land or language . . . Things like courage, sacrifice, a passion for freedom, and all that . . . There is a fascination about a man — whoever he is, wherever, and no matter his color — who has the courage of his convictions . . . who is willing to die for them . . . Perhaps that was the attraction, the basis of what you call his hold on me."

"I can understand that, Ilka," Leighton said. "Nevertheless, my dear, Singh killed a man. And he has to face the consequences. Knowing him, his courage, his fanatical patriotism, I have no doubt he will face them willingly without flinching."

"And so, I hope, shall I," Ilka said quietly.

Leighton turned and grasped both her wrists. His usually kind and soft gray eyes had a glint of steel in them she had never seen before. He was no longer desperate but determined. If she could not quite make up her mind, she saw before he spoke that he had made up his.

"Ilka, they will be here in a moment or two. I shall do the talking. Is that understood?"

She gazed at him wonderingly. "You can't face it, can you, darling?" she said.

"Face what?"

"Why not say it? . . . That I was an accomplice!"

He gulped, but she could see that he was very much in control of himself.

"No, Ilka," he said determinedly, "I'm afraid I can't face it — at least not squarely. So far as I'm concerned, you had nothing to do with it. Singh just walked in here, so completely disguised that you couldn't possibly have recognized him, and opened fire. That's what you've said all week. And we're going to stick to it."

"But it isn't true!"

"It has to be true!"

"The truth is . . . I helped!"

"How could you have helped! It's a hallucination, Ilka!"

"I will tell you," Ilka said quietly . . . "if you will listen at last. I . . ."

"No! I don't want to hear!"

"But you have to, Harold! I have to get it off my chest, first to you — and then, to them!"

"You imagine it all! You have a feverish imagination, Ilka!"

"Let me tell you, Harold," she said slowly, almost whispering the words . . . "what I did — what actually happened."

"No!" Leighton turned away. He stood up and strode across the room and then swung around to face her. "I tell you it's a hallucination! . . . You imagine it all! . . . For what reason, God knows!"

Ilka walked slowly to her desk and picked up her notes.

"If you prefer, read this," she said, holding the papers out to him. "It's all here, Harold — in black and white — just as it happened, from beginning to end."

Leighton took the notes, glanced at the top page and then slowly folded the bundle in two.

"No, my dear . . . I don't want to read it . . ." He started to hand the notes back, hesitated, and then began to crumple them between his sweating hands.

"We must destroy them!" he cried. "This instant!"

"Harold! No!"

Ilka tried to snatch the papers from him but Harold had turned. He was muttering wildly to himself and darting about the room. ". . . If we had a fireplace it would be easy . . . Here! Maybe this will do!" He picked up a great copper bowl which she had emptied of its fading flowers but a few hours ago. ". . . We will burn it in this! . . ." He paused to look out past the veranda, to the driveway and then at his watch. He stuffed the papers in the bowl and reached in his pocket for his lighter. "We'll do one page at a time . . . just to make sure! . . ." He seized the crumpled papers, snatched a sheet and held his lighter to it.

Ilka ran over to him, but he warded her off with his back.

"Harold! You can't! I beg you!"

"There's not much time!" The first sheet had burned down to his finger tips and he let it fall into the bowl. He grabbed another.

"It's too cowardly! . . . Stop!" Ilka tried to step around him to tear the pages out of his left hand, but he swerved and again warded her off.

"Now! I will have them out of the way in a moment, my dear! No one will ever know! . . ."

Ilka felt limp. She stood there behind him helplessly and finally stepped slowly back and sank on the divan, watching him listlessly. When he turned halfway, holding up a flaming sheet and waving it until it was consumed, she could see his face contorted with a strange Mephistophelean grin. The acrid odor of burning paper nauseated her.

"Burn some incense, Ilka!" Harold called out.

Mechanically she got up and went to the desk, opened a drawer, took out a box of incense, picked out three pieces, distributed them in ash trays about the room and lit them.

This modest, decent man, then, had triumphed over her in his turn, as Singh had in his — she who had always felt herself so strong and dominant. That must be the way it was fated to be. This mildest of men, she saw, would flinch at nothing, when the instant of supreme crisis came, to save her, as he thought, and of course to save himself. On his part, it was a sheer act of self-preservation, an instinct deeper than all the others one had. It was more than that, of course. Mixed in it was nobility, loyalty, love. She knew that he, like Singh, would have sacrificed himself, his strict probity, his very life, to spare her. And that, undoubtedly, in the heat of this awful moment was what he was utterly convinced he was doing. She did not question the purity of his heart; one had to stoop to deceit occasionally in this imperfect world to accomplish what was important in one's life, and to ward off disaster. What Harold would never understand was that she was beyond saving by any act of his. She would have her remorse, her gnawing sense of guilt, to carry to the last breath. The evil she had done could have been atoned for, in part at least, if he had allowed her to do what she had wished. But then — there was no way out of the dilemma — he would have been destroyed. Would that be enough to live for — the realization that at least she had saved him from that? Life demanded sacrifice. Did she not owe this one to him?

She watched him holding up the last pages to the flames. In a fortnight this place, this haunted room, would be only a memory, though an indelible one that would not ever fade very far from her mind. They would be in the mountains of Tyrol, the scene of her first breath-less days of marriage to this man before the experiences of adult life had begun to shape the destiny that had led to so sorry an end. The marriage, the first happy, full days in Austria, had released her from the oppressive memories of her youth in savage revolutionary Buda-pest. But she had not really escaped from what had torn men apart along the Danube. In so many other places, and finally here in Pawancore, there had been the same inhumanity of man; and as at first in her native city, now at last here in this steaming, unhappy land, she had been caught up in it. And she had been stained by its blood. Only the timid or the lucky escaped.

Harold Leighton had finished with his burning.

"That's that," he said. He was grasping the smoking urn. "I shall leave it in the bathroom upstairs. The in-cense smells good, Ilka. They will never suspect. I shall go wash my hands. My dear, if you hear them coming, call me first. I shall be down in a moment."

Ilka sat back in the divan and lit a cigarette. At least, she thought, for the first time in weeks she was no longer torn by indecision. She would let Harold do the talking, as he insisted. Neither he nor Singh would ever under-stand. But it was all becoming very clear to her. What had happened here in this spot could be justified. Never-theless, it had to be paid for. She did not flinch from facing that. Singh would pay in full — and willingly

[253]

and bravely. Harold, out of the goodness of his heart, believed he could save her from paying her share; but he was wrong. Her punishment — the crushing load on her heart, on her mind — was just beginning and it was a sentence for life.

Chapter 17

THE TYROL that late summer was as lovely as they had ever known it in their younger days. The usual rains held off. The days were bathed in warm sunshine, and as the sun moved across the clear, blue skies above the mountains it cast a dozen hues of green upon the valleys and upon the woods of evergreens that ran steeply up from them toward the glistening, snowy peaks. Always there was a nip in the air that the Leightons had not felt for years and the nights, under the starry skies, were blessedly cool.

Ilka was pleased to see her husband making such a rapid recovery. His sense of relief at getting her out of Pawancore unscathed had been so overwhelming that he had suffered an inevitable reaction on arriving here and his relapse had been aggravated by a return of malaria. They had put him to bed, but now after a fortnight he was up and about and talking of joining her and Bob Snow on some of their climbing expeditions.

Isobel had gone off to Paris. She had wanted, she said, to think things over for herself before deciding what she would do: whether she would return home with them in the fall, stay in Europe, or go back to Asia. For Leighton, she had been almost as much of a problem the last week in Pawancore as Ilka. She had declined to leave — at least until Singh's fate was sealed. But his court-martial had been postponed: his questioning would go on for some time, the acting governor had told Leighton. In the end, he had persuaded Isobel to accompany them only by promising that she could go off by herself to Paris and make her own decision. Once in Europe and, as he hoped, eventually in America, she would gradually get over, he was sure, her grim desire to return to Pawancore. By that time, Singh would have met his end.

That Singh would carry Ilka's secret to the grave he had no doubt. Ilka had not mentioned him here. She seemed to Leighton to be recuperating from her dreadful ordeal very well. She had played the game with him loyally to the very last. The final afternoon of questioning had been the easiest of all their interrogations. Ilka had let him do almost all the talking. And when she had to answer, she had stuck bravely to her original story. Still, he had not breathed easily until they were safely on the plane and making their first landing in India.

The thought of what might have happened to her still gave him bad dreams. Even here in the coolness of the mountains, with the fever receding and his old stamina sprouting back, he had awakened at least twice in a cold sweat to cut short a nightmare in which he had watched her being taken off in chains to the malaria islands. That is what they would have done to her, despite her position — and his. He had visited those islands once and seen the living skeletons slowly wasting away with fever. Even the kind of death that lay in store for Singh was preferable to the protracted dying on the dreaded islands. But he never could have faced either kind for Ilka. He was not man enough for that. She seemed to understand his weakness. That was one reason, certainly, why she had complied with his demands, though in his desperation he would have enforced them somehow, regardless.

Soon, in a few weeks, both of them would come down to earth and bury, as far as possible, the immediate past. Leighton began to think of what lay ahead. Senator Bridgehorn, abetted by Chester Groves, had done his best, he knew, to hasten his retirement. But apparently they had failed. In the fall he would be back at a desk in Washington — a strange but welcome experience for him. Perhaps in his new post he would still be able to exert some influence on the future of Pawancore. He would keep after the Secretary, as he had from the consulate, to maintain pressure on the British to turn over the country to the people, as they were obviously going to do in India . . .

One sunny morning toward the end of August, he and Ilka and Snow set off up the valley towards a peak they had talked of climbing before they left. They would reconnoiter a little and have a picnic lunch on the edge of the woods at the tree line. They had been depressed all the previous day. The morning newspaper from Innsbruck had carried a three-line item on the next to the last page. The Pawancore terrorist Govind Singh, it said, the confessed slayer of the late governor-general, had been hanged in Pawancore City.

Ilka had lain prostrate on her bed all the rest of the day. Leighton and Snow had not disturbed her. But Snow had insisted that they go for a long hike the next day. Bob was doing his best, Leighton realized, to help restore both of them to some semblance of their former selves. If only by some miracle life could be turned back to where it had really started for Ilka and him in this mountainous paradise on their honeymoon a quarter of a century ago! The thought made him smile. In truth, he had no desire to live his life over again. Even to muse about it gave him a feeling of fatigue, of weariness. He felt relieved that the strenuous years were about over. No doubt, if they could relive them, they would make the same mistakes — or comparable ones. Perhaps if they could do over again the last years in Pawancore, he might avoid the last fatal blunder, but he was not even sure of that. The courses taken by the lives of human beings, even of those you knew and loved, even of your own, were as unpredictable and sometimes as far beyond one's control as the dizzy paths of the comets.

Sometimes there was bound to be a hideous clash. What was important for mortals was to be able to recover from no matter how hard a blow.

Under the bright sun, which was so much kinder than the one that scorched Pawancore, the three of them that forenoon made their way up the valley toward the mountain. In the long, narrow fields the peasants were getting in some late hay and the sweet odor of the freshly mown meadows permeated the air. Sometimes the hikers paused to glance up at the peak ahead half covered in snow. Its pink hue of the early morning was paling and by noon it would be pure white and sparkling against the deep blue sky. Striding single-file up the narrow, rocky path they were mostly silent, each of the three buried in thought.

Bob Snow was thinking of all he had gone through with the other two, of how their love and friendship had endured and of how fine it would be to have them back home at last and for good. He knew something of the loneliness of the foreign service officer, condemned by the nature of his calling to spend his life so cut off from the effervescence of his native land that he was in danger of becoming alien to it. He had no doubt that Harold would make the readjustment to living and working at home gracefully and intelligently. Washington was full of plodding, worried, mediocre, time-serving men, and to those who knew him, Leighton would be a welcome addition to the capital and especially to the Department, swarming as the latter was with careful, unimaginative, meticulous little creatures.

Ilka, too, Snow was sure, would get to like it there. For one thing, there would be for her some tranquillity. At the moment that was what she most needed. Later on her old restlessness would doubtless return, but in America, and in Washington above all, there would be plenty of normal outlets for that. In the steaming heat and turbulence of Pawancore there had seemingly been only a tragic one. He was not attempting to judge her for what she had done there. She must have found some justification for helping to kill a man whom she felt — and not without reason — had the blood of so many innocent beings on his hands. Whatever her guilt she deserved to live; they had been right to get her out of the hell of Pawancore safely.

Snow watched her ambling gracefully along just ahead of him. When she turned sometimes to glance across the valley she seemed to him to be as fresh and lovely as she had appeared long ago when they had first come up to the mountains from Vienna. Her black eyes were just as full of mystery. In all the years he had not penetrated it very far. Had Harold? Singh? He wondered.

As they plodded along, Harold Leighton was thinking of Ilka too. He felt thankful to the Almighty that she had been spared. There would still be some good years ahead for them. From now on he would not have to devote so much of his energies and his time to his work.

There would be more time for her, more opportunity to draw closer to her and to try to better fathom the well-springs that lay so deep within her. There would never be an end to getting to know this strange and beautiful woman. The image of her the first time they had come to these mountains at the time of their wedding kept coming back to him. Yet it blurred so easily into the sight of her now. There was the same haunting beauty and the same exciting mystery.

A good many thoughts kept running through Ilka Leighton as they trudged leisurely along. How did Singh face the end? Did they clamp a black hood on him at the last? So that none could see the smile, the serenity? There must have been a light in his handsome, sensitive face. It must have been like the one she had seen when he had turned on her one day after she had warned him of what might happen if he persisted in going ahead. "My dear madame," he had said, "if freedom is to be won, somebody has to be ready to die for it." There was a man! And whatever gnawing there would always be at her heart for her responsibility in the cruel denouement of his life, she was grateful to the fates which had arranged for her to know him and to share with him this last shattering experience.

Singh was dead, and she must go on living. Harold too was a noble man and he had sustained her selflessly even when, at the end, their roads parted. The fork she had taken with Singh had come to an end. She must go back now and take the other turning. In a few weeks it would mean resuming the role of the diplomat's wife . . . tea parties and bridge . . . cocktails and gossip . . . with all the turmoil of sweating, yearning men, of patriot-assassins dangling from the gallows, of governors being slain, no longer to be seen or experienced or shared but merely noticed from time to time in the cold print of a newspaper or in the dulcet tones of a voice on the radio, as if such sufferings occurred on another planet.

Five years of it in the tedious atmosphere of Washington and then — hadn't Harold said? — a peaceful retirement in the country, on some little farm in Virginia or Vermont. Well, if that were to be her fate, so be it. She would carry her burden as gracefully and as far from the surface as possible and spare others, those whom she loved, Harold above all, from being afflicted by her agony. That, however, would be a negative course. Was there no possibility of adding something affirmative? She had helped extinguish the life of one man — and indeed of a second. It remained for her to sustain the life of a third. Perhaps if she did it well, that would be part of the atonement she had been prevented from making. She would try.

She quickened her step and caught up with Harold. The path through the last stretch of pine as they neared the tree line widened. His breath seemed a little short and a slight pallor was coming over his face from the exertion. She took his arm and helped him gently along toward the clearing. Beyond they could glimpse the steep rocky slope of the mountain. It would be difficult, Ilka thought, but when he was well they would climb it.